THE CASUALTY

The Casualty

HEINRICH BÖLL

Translated from the German by
LEILA VENNEWITZ

Chatto & Windus
London

57943

Published in 1986 by
Chatto & Windus Ltd
40 William IV Street
London WC2N 4DF

British Library Cataloguing in Publication Data
Böll, Heinrich
    The Casualty
    I. Title II. Die Verwundung. *English*
    833'.914 [F]   PT2603.0394

ISBN 0 7011 2928 X

First published in 1983 in Germany as *Die Verwundung*

Die Verwundung Copyright © 1983 Lamuv Verlag GmbH
English translation Copyright © 1986 by Leila Vennewitz
and the Estate of Heinrich Böll

Typeset at The Spartan Press Ltd
Lymington, Hants
Printed in Great Britain by
Redwood Burn Ltd
Trowbridge, Wiltshire

Contents

This translation, to which my husband has brought
his knowledge, patience and skill, was made
in memory of the author, who died 16 July 1985

The Translator

The Embrace

He was looking down on the parting in her hair, a narrow white path; he felt her breasts against his skin, her warm breath in his face, and his gaze fell into the endless distance of that narrow white path. Somewhere on the carpet lay his belt with, clearly visible, the embossed words: GOTT MIT UNS; beside it his tunic with its soiled collarband, and somewhere a clock was ticking.

The window was open, and from outside on the terrace he could hear the tinkle of fine crystal, hear men chuckling and women giggling. The sky was a velvet blue; it was a glorious summer night.

And he could hear her heart beating, very close to his chest, and again his gaze fell into that narrow white path through her hair.

It was dark, but the sky still held that soft summer glow, and he knew he was close to her, as close as he could be, while still so infinitely remote. They didn't say a word. The clock seemed to be ticking him away, the ticking was stronger than the heartbeat against his chest, and he couldn't tell whether it was her heart or his. The message was: you're on leave until reveille; and: one more chance to sleep with a girl, but make a real night of it. They had even given him a bottle of wine.

He could distinctly make out the bottle as it stood on the chest of drawers, a bright band of light. That was the bottle, a bright band of light in the dark. The bottle was empty. The cork must be on the carpet, where his tunic, trousers and belt were lying.

She had lain against his chest, he with one arm round her

and smoking with his free hand; they hadn't said a word. All their encounters were marked by silence. He had always thought it might sometimes be possible to talk to a woman, but she never talked.

Outside the sky darkened, the subdued laughter of the guests on the terrace faded away, the women's giggles turned into yawns, and after a while he could hear the glasses clinking louder as the waiter picked up four or five in one hand to carry them away. Then the bottles were being taken away too, making a fuller sound, and finally chairs were upended, tables moved, and he could hear a woman sweeping slowly, thoroughly, conscientiously: the entire night seemed to consist of that sweeping as she swept with a quiet, regular stroke. He could hear the sweep of the broom and the woman's footsteps moving from one end of the terrace to the other; then came a weary, thick voice asking from beyond a door: 'Not finished yet?', and the woman's reply, equally weary: 'I'll be through in a minute.'

Soon after that, complete silence fell; the sky had turned dark blue. Softly and from very far away came the sound of music from behind the heavy curtains of a night club. So they lay side by side, until the empty bottle slowly emerged from the darkness, a band of light growing wider and brighter until the bottle assumed its full, round shape, dark green and empty, and the tunic on the floor with its soiled collarband became visible, and the belt with the embossed words: GOTT MIT UNS.

The Unknown Soldier

Somewhere up ahead was where the front began. He kept thinking they had reached it whenever the truck column slowed down and stopped in a village, where corporals and soldiers with grim, set faces were moving about in dirt and mud. But the journey was always resumed, and he was scared because for a while now they had been hearing shots close by. They must have already moved beyond the emplacements of the heavy artillery since the detonations were now coming from behind, where the column had just come from. But on they went. It was cold, and it was no use to keep trying to pull one's greatcoat closer or tugging at the collar as if it could be made longer. And their gloves were too thin, and he didn't even feel like smoking: he was simply too cold, as well as horribly tired.

His eyes kept closing, but nausea kept him from falling asleep. He was sickened by the exhaust fumes, and it made him uneasy that no one in the truck said a word. Normally their tongues never stopped wagging. Even while they were in the troop train, on their way here, they had talked all day, about their women and their exploits and about their fancy flats back home and their important jobs. There wasn't one of them who didn't have a gorgeous flat and a super job, but now they were all terribly quiet, and he could tell from their breathing that they were shivering with cold. The road was rough, the mud over a foot deep, rutted by tank tracks, with here and there the imprint of a horse's hoof. The poor horses, he thought. And he didn't even think of the infantrymen who had to slog it on foot. It was great to be driven, but it would have been better to walk, it would have warmed them up and they wouldn't have got there so fast.

But now he wanted to get there faster. He really did feel as sick as a dog. With each breath he seemed to inhale new nausea. He could smell not only the stink of the exhaust right under his nose but also the stench of the men sitting behind him, all of whom – including himself – hadn't had a proper wash for a couple of weeks, just hands and faces. A foul miasma of sour, disgusting, dirty, stale sweat came from behind him. Some of the men were smoking; he was ready to throw up and would have welcomed it if someone had taken pity on him, held a service revolver to his head, and pressed the trigger . . .

And still they hadn't reached the front. Now he could hear the firing of the machine guns, so close that he felt they must be driving right into it. The village they were passing through looked exactly as he imagined a front-line village to look. Soldiers with muddy boots and the totally deadpan faces of heroes, wearing their decorations and staring straight ahead, and corporals who no longer looked so much like corporals; and some lieutenants, and a field kitchen behind a filthy cottage, in a yard apparently consisting solely of manure and mud. But they were soon through the godforsaken hole and still they hadn't quite reached the front. Goddammit, he thought, where the hell's the infantry?

They stopped beside a small forest that covered a hill. Somewhere up front a voice roared 'Everybody out!' and he immediately jumped down from the lorry and began to stamp his feet to get warm. The others tossed out the baggage, and he had to catch not only a machine gun but also the ammunition boxes, which he dropped in the mud. The corporal, pale-faced and shivering, gave him hell for dropping the boxes in the mud. He looked in astonishment at the corporal. What the hell difference did it make? As far as he was concerned they could shoot him on the spot if they felt like it. He simply felt too wretched to care.

He grabbed his rifle, combat pack, and two boxes of ammunition, and stepped into the bushes after hearing the order from up front: 'Get off the road!' It was wet in the bushes, some of the men were smoking, and he fished a cigarette out of his pocket. He saw everything and heard everything, yet he heard and saw nothing: the sky was grey all over, without a single dark or light speck, and it must be about five in the afternoon. The soldiers hunkered down on their boxes; some of them were stamping around, but they soon gave up because the ground was too soft and wet, so wet that it splashed when they stamped on it.

Nothing much was said. Somewhere the NCOs were gathered round the lieutenant, and on the path leading into the forest a captain appeared with a list. He was a young captain who for some reason snapped at the lieutenant, and the lieutenant stood to attention. The noise of machine guns started up again: the gunner couldn't have been lying more than ten yards away. Then came the sound of quite a different machine gun, and he knew that that rough, slower, throaty sound must come from the Russian machine guns. For a moment he felt his terrible indifference shot through with something like excitement. The captain in his muddy boots with his incredibly young face was now talking urgently to the lieutenant and the NCOs.

He threw away his cigarette and turned to the man nearest to him. It was cold; he looked at him, and it was some time before he realized that it was Karl – Karl, that quiet, inconspicuous fellow who hadn't had much to say

11

on the journey, an older man wearing a wedding ring who had always seemed a pillar of respectability.

'Karl,' he said in a low voice.

'What is it?' Karl answered quietly.

'Got anything to drink?' Karl nodded and fumbled at the canteen hanging from his belt.

He groped for the stopper with one hand, unscrewed it, and lifted the canteen to his mouth, and when the first gulp ran down his throat he was suddenly aware of having a hellish thirst. He groaned with pleasure and drank deeply.

Suddenly their corporal shouted 'Fall in!' and Karl hurriedly snatched back his canteen and hooked it on again. All the sections were being called by their corporals, assembled on the forest path, then marched off in rows behind the captain into the forest.

All he could think of was drinking.

His thirst was barbaric: he was tempted to throw himself on the ground and drink the puddle on the path. The forest path seemed familiar. This thin, scrubby growth, these skimpy little beech trees standing far apart, and between them the brown, sodden earth; the grey, endlessly grey sky overhead, and this squelchy path. Up ahead the captain, talking earnestly to the lieutenant, and the corporals beside their sections: just like on the training ground when they used to march off for firing practice . . . it was all nonsense, they weren't really in Russia, they hadn't covered all those thousands of kilometres by train to be shot up here or to freeze to death. It was all a dream.

The firing ahead of them sounded regular and familiar: rifles and machine guns, somewhere artillery too.

Suddenly they halted. He looked up to find they were standing in front of a hut hidden in the trees beside the path. Behind it were more huts, and deeper inside the forest

12

he could see holes in the ground, entrances to dug-outs hung with blankets and telephone cables, and somewhere in a dilapidated shed stood a field kitchen. Once again they had to leave the path and step under the scrawny little trees. Troopers emerged from the dug-outs, and some corporals and another lieutenant. They seemed quite unconcerned, and he thought: so it's not Russia after all. Everything was so terribly normal. The trooper who joined them had a machine pistol slung over one shoulder and a pipe stuck in his grey face. He had always imagined that, when they reached the front, the real front, they would be looked at with contempt as being greenhorns. But no one looked contemptuously at them; in fact they seemed rather indifferent, if anything a bit sorry for them.

What a marvellous war-game they're having here, he thought. Everything's so incredibly real, I hope the shooting's real too and they'll shoot me dead. His nausea had not subsided; his head ached, and a sour, horrible sick feeling rose from his stomach into his head and seemed to fill all his veins and nerves. He took deep breaths – the fresh air felt good for at least a tenth of a second. They're playing a damn convincing game, he thought, as the trooper who had joined them walked right up to the corporal and said: 'To the third.'

'Yessir!' replied the corporal, and the trooper gave him an odd look. 'Okay, let's go,' said the trooper, and he marched off into the forest, followed by the corporal and the men in single file.

Carrying his ammunition box, he was the last but one. He staggered along behind the man in front of him, through that sparse beech wood, feeling miserably cold, sick to his stomach . . .

Suddenly their guide, the trooper, threw himself on the

13

ground shouting 'Take cover!' and at that very moment
some shells burst in front of them. It couldn't be far away: he
heard a sickening soft rustling, a rush of wind, then the
crash, and one of the little beech trees snapped right off and
fell over. He could clearly see a slender tree trunk bursting
twenty yards away and slowly toppling over, revealing its
white, greenish-white, core at the place of impact. Clods of
earth rained down, some of them splattering the ground
close by. It was wonderful to be lying on the ground.
Although he knew very well that this was for real, that they
were in Russia, actually in Russia, and almost right up at the
very front, all he felt was: how wonderful to be lying on the
ground, full length. Although it was wet and the cold and
damp quickly penetrated his greatcoat, he simply didn't
care.

Dear God, he prayed, let the next shell land right on top of
me . . . But the trooper was back on his feet, shouting 'Let's
go!' On they marched and soon they reached the edge of the
forest. The trooper waited until they were all there and then
explained something to them. He could hear it all quite
distinctly, but he couldn't have cared less about any of it;
never in his life had he felt so utterly indifferent. Moreover,
by this time he was so cold that his teeth were chattering.
Before them was a big field, all torn up, and on it a burned-
out tank with a Soviet star painted on its side. On either side
of the tank were emplacements. It looked exactly like the
training area. Proper trenches and dug-out mounds, and he
saw which machine gun was firing – it seemed to sound
much farther away than it had a while ago when they had
been in the lorry. And the machine gun was firing at the
remains of a house standing at the end of the field: he saw
the impacts, saw the mud spray up from the ruined walls,
and from an entirely different direction a throaty-sounding,

slower machine gun was now firing at the edge of the forest just where they were standing. The trooper, their leader, threw himself on the ground again, and they didn't wait for him to shout 'Take cover!' for one of them had been hit and lay there screaming, screaming horribly, and the machine gun went on firing.

He was about to slide over to his mate, realizing from the voice that it was Willi, but two men were already lying on their stomachs beside Willi, bandaging one leg. He distinctly heard one of the bullets smash into a tender young sapling. A few ricochet bullets buzzed into the void like demented bees.

When he saw the others cautiously crawling backwards, he did the same, although his fatigue and nausea made everything swim before his eyes. It was exhausting work, pushing oneself backwards, and the machine gun was now sawing right above their heads; it was horrifying the way the bullets were slapping into the forest floor behind them or into the soft wood, revealing the young, greenish-white wounds. And then another shell burst, then several more; everything was reduced to noise and a horrible stench, and again a man screamed, then another. He didn't know who was screaming, all he wanted was to sleep; he closed his eyes and screamed, went on screaming without knowing that he was screaming, until God granted his wish . . .

Jak the Tout

He arrived one night with the ration runners as a replacement for Gornizek, who lay wounded at battalion head-
quarters. Those nights were very dark, and fear hung like a
thunder cloud over the alien, pitch-black earth. I was up
front at a listening post, keeping my eyes and ears open
towards the rear, from where the sounds of the ration
runners came, just as much as towards the front, towards
the dark silence on the Russian side.

It was Gerhard who brought him along, together with my
mess-tin and cigarettes.

'D'you want the bread, too?' Gerhard asked, 'or shall I
keep it for you till tomorrow morning?' I could tell from his
voice that he was in a hurry to get back.

'No,' I said, 'give me the lot, it'll be eaten up right away.'

He handed me the bread and the tinned meat in a piece of
wax paper, the roll of fruit-drops and some mixed butter
and lard on a scrap of cardboard.

All this time the newcomer had been standing there
trembling and silent. 'And here,' said Gerhard, 'is the
replacement for Gornizek. The lieutenant has sent him out
to you, to the listening post.'

'Yes,' was all I said; it was customary to send newcomers
to the most difficult posts. Gerhard crawled back to the rear.

'Come on down,' I said quietly. 'Not so much noise, for
God's sake!' He was making a stupid racket with the stuff
hanging from his belt, his spade and gas mask; he stepped
clumsily into the hole and almost knocked over my mess-
tin. 'Idiot,' I muttered as I made room for him. I heard
rather than saw how he proceeded to unbuckle his belt,

place the spade to one side, his gas mask beside it, and his rifle up onto the parapet, pointing at the enemy, and then buckle on his belt again, all strictly according to regulations.

The bean soup was cold by this time, and it was just as well that in the dark I couldn't see all the grubs that must have been boiled out of the beans. There was plenty of meat in the soup, delicious crisp brown bits. Next I ate up the tinned meat from the wax paper and stuffed the bread into the empty mess-tin. He stood perfectly silent beside me, always facing the enemy, and in the blackness of the night I could see a snub-nosed profile. When he turned aside, I could tell from his narrow cheeks that he was still young; his steel helmet looked almost like the shell of a tortoise. These boys had a special something about their cheeks that recalled playing soldiers on a suburban common. 'My Redskin brother,' they always seemed to be saying, and their lips trembled with fear, and their hearts were stiff with courage. Those poor kids . . .

'You might as well sit down,' I said in that painstakingly acquired voice that is easily intelligible but scarcely audible a yard away. 'Here,' I added, pulling at the hem of his greatcoat and almost forcing him down into the hollowed-out seat. 'You can't possibly stand all the time.'

'But on sentry duty . . .' came a feeble voice that cracked like that of a sentimental tenor.

'Shut up!' I hissed at him.

'But on sentry duty,' he whispered, 'we're not permitted to sit!'

'Nothing's permitted, not even starting a war.'

Although I could see him only in outline, I knew that he was now sitting like a pupil in class, hands on knees, bolt upright and ready to jump up any second. I bent forward,

17

drew my greatcoat right over the back of my head, and lit my pipe.

'Want a smoke?'

'No.' I was surprised how quickly he had learned to whisper.

'Well, anyway,' I said, 'have a drink instead.'

'No,' he repeated, but I grabbed his head and held the neck of the flask to his mouth; as patient as a calf with its first bottle, he swallowed a few times, then made such a violent gesture of disgust that I took away the flask.

'Don't you like it?'

'I do,' he stammered, 'but I choked.'

'Then drink it yourself.'

He took the flask out of my hand and swallowed a good gulp.

'Thanks,' he murmured. I had a drink, too.

'Feeling better now?'

'Yes – much.'

'Not quite so scared, eh?'

He was ashamed to admit that he was scared at all, but they were all like that.

'I'm scared, too,' I said, 'all the time, that's why I find courage in a bottle.'

I felt him jerk towards me, and I leaned over to see his face. All I could see was the bright glint of his eyes, eyes that looked dangerous, and shadowy dark outlines, but I could smell him. He smelled of army stores, of sweat, storeroom, and leftover soup, and slightly of the schnapps. There was no sound at all; behind us they seemed to have finished doling out the rations. He turned back towards the enemy.

'Is this your first time out?'

Again he was ashamed, I could tell, but he answered: 'Yes.'

'How long have you been a soldier?'

'Eight weeks.'

'And where are you from?'

'From St Avold.'

'Where?'

'St Avold. Lorraine, you know . . .'

'A long trip?'

'Two weeks.'

We fell silent, and I tried to peer through the impenetrable darkness ahead. Oh, if only daylight would come, I thought, if one could at least see something, daybreak at least, some fog maybe – see something, see anything, a scrap of light . . . but when daylight came I would be wishing that it was dark. If only dusk would fall, or fog would roll in suddenly. It was always the same . . .

Up front there was nothing. Off in the distance, the gentle throbbing of engines. The Russians were being fed, too. Then came the sound of a twittering Russian voice that was abruptly suppressed, as if a hand had been clapped over a mouth. It was nothing . . .

'Do you know what our job is?' I asked him. How good it felt not to be alone any more! How wonderful to feel the breath of a human being, to be aware of his stale smell – a human being who was not about to finish one off the very next second!

'Yes,' he said, 'listening post.' Again I was surprised how well he could whisper, almost better than I could. It seemed so effortless. For me it was always an effort, I always wanted to shout, yell, call out, so that the night would collapse like black foam; for me it was a terrible effort, that whispering.

'Fine,' I said, 'listening post. So we have to be on the look-out for when the Russians come, when they attack. Then we send up a red flare, bang away with our rifles for a bit, and scram, to the rear – got it? But when only a few come, a recce patrol, then we have to keep quiet, let them through, and one of us has to go back and tell the others, tell the lieutenant – you've been in his dug-out, haven't you?'

'Yes,' he said, his voice trembling.

'Okay. And if the patrol attacks us both, then we have to finish them off, dead as doornails, right? We mustn't clear out just for a patrol. Got it? Okay?'

'Yes,' he said, his voice still trembling, and then I heard a dreadful sound: his teeth were chattering.

'Here,' I said, handing him the flask.

I had another drink, too.

'But suppose . . . suppose . . .' he stammered, 'suppose we can't even see them coming . . .'

'Then we're done for. But don't worry – we're bound to see them or hear them. And if we suspect something we're allowed to send up a flare, then we'll see everything.' He was silent again; it was terrible the way he was never the first to speak.

'But they won't come,' I rattled on, 'they never come at night. If they come at all, it'll be in the morning, two minutes before dawn . . .'

'Two minutes before dawn?' he broke in.

'Two minutes before dawn is when they start, then they'll be here by first light . . .'

'But then surely it's too late.'

'Well, then we have to quickly send up a red flare and clear out – don't worry, you'll find you can run like a hare. And don't forget we'll hear it first. What's your name, anyway?' It was a nuisance, every time I wanted to speak to him I had to nudge him, take my hands out of my warm pockets and stuff them back in and wait till they got warm again . . .

'My name,' he said, 'my name's Jak.'

'English?'

'No,' he said, 'it's from Jakob . . . Jak a-k, not Jack – Jak, just Jak.'

'Jak,' I went on, 'what did you do for a living?'

'Me? My last job was as a tout.'

'What's that?'

'A tout.'

'What did you tout then?'

He jerked his face towards me, and I could tell he was very surprised.

'What did I tout – what did I tout? Well, I was just a tout!'

'What d'you mean? *What* did you tout?'

He was silent for a while, looking straight ahead again; then in the darkness his head turned back towards me.

'Well,' he said, 'I was touting,' and he sighed deeply. 'I stood at the railway station, towards the end anyway, and when someone came, came by, in that crowd someone I thought might be interested, most of them were soldiers of course – so when someone came by I'd ask him in a low voice, a very low voice, you know: "Want a good time, sir?" That's what I'd ask . . .' His voice was trembling again, and this time it may not have been fear but recollection.

In my eagerness I forgot to take a drink. 'And,' I asked hoarsely, 'if he did want to have a good time?'

'Then,' he said with an effort, and again it seemed to be the recollection that overcame him, 'then I'd take him to whichever one of the girls happened to be free.'

'To a cathouse, you mean?'

'No,' he said matter-of-factly, 'I wasn't working for the cathouses, I had a few freelancers, you know, a few loners who kept me going. Three without a license. Irma, Lilli and Amadea . . .'

21

'Amadea?' I broke in.

'Right, that was her name. Funny, eh? She used to tell me that her father had wanted a son and he'd have called him Amadeus so that's why he called her Amadea. Funny, eh?' He actually managed a little laugh.

We had both forgotten why we were sitting in that filthy hole. And now I no longer had to pump him: he rattled away without any help from me.

'Amadea,' he went on, 'was the nicest. She was always generous and sad and really the prettiest, too, and . . .'

'So,' I interrupted him, 'you were actually a pimp, weren't you?'

'No,' he carefully explained, 'no,' and he sighed again. 'Pimps – they're biggies, they're tyrants, they make heaps of money, and they sleep with the girls too.'

'And you didn't?'

'No, I was only a tout. It was my job to hook the fish for them to fry and eat, then they'd give me some of the bones to pick . . .'

'The bones?'

'Yes.' He gave a short laugh. 'Just a tip, see? And that's what I lived on after my dad was killed and my mother disappeared. I wasn't fit to work, see, because of my lung. No, the girls I worked for didn't have a pimp, thank God. Otherwise I'd have got beaten up all the time. No, they just worked for themselves, all on their own, no license or anything, and they didn't dare show up in the street like the others – that was too dangerous, so I touted for them.' He sighed. 'Mind passing me the bottle again?' While I was reaching down to pick up the bottle, he asked: 'And what's your name?'

'Hubert,' I said, handing him the bottle.

'That feels good,' he said, but I couldn't respond because

by then I was holding the bottle to my lips. It was empty, and I let it roll gently to one side.

'Hubert,' he suddenly said, and now his voice was trembling violently, 'look!' He pulled me forward to where he was lying flat on the parapet. 'Just look!' If one looked very, very hard one could see very, very far away something like a horizon, a pitch-black line with a suspicion of light over it, and in the lighter darkness above the pitch-black line something was moving like a gentle motion of bushes. It could also be men creeping up, a huge mass of men creeping up without a sound . . .

'Why don't you send up a white flare?' he whispered in an expiring voice.

'Listen,' I said, placing my hand on his shoulder. 'Jak, it's nothing, it's just our fear that's moving out there, it's all that hell, it's the war, it's all that shit that's driving us crazy – it's – it's not real.'

'But I can see it, I'm sure it's something – something real –they're coming – they're coming . . .' And again I could hear his teeth chattering.

'Yes,' I said, 'be quiet. It *is* something real. It's sunflower stalks, in the morning you'll see them and laugh, when it's broad daylight you'll see and you'll laugh, it's sunflower stalks, they're about half a mile away, and they look as if they're at the end of the world, don't they? I know them – dried up, black, dirty, some of them shot to pieces, and the Russians have eaten the pods, and it's our fear that's making them move.'

'Please – please send up a white flare – send up a flare – I can see them!'

'But I know what they are, Jak!'

'Please send up a flare! Just one single shell . . .'

'Come on, Jak,' I whispered back, 'if they were really

23

coming we could hear them – listen!' We held our breath and listened. There was complete silence, nothing to be heard except those ghastly sounds of silence.

'I hear them,' he whispered, and I could tell from his voice that he was deathly pale, 'I do hear them – they're coming – they're creeping – they're crawling over the ground – there, a clink! They're coming very silently, and when they're close up it'll be too late . . .'

'Jak,' I said, 'I can't shoot off a flare, I've only two cartridges, understand? And I'll need one in the morning, very early, when the Stukas come, so they know where we are and don't bomb us to hell. And the other one – I'll need that when things really get hot. In the morning you'll be laughing . . .'

'In the morning,' he said without emotion. 'Tomorrow morning I'll be dead.' I was so taken aback that I swung round to him. He had spoken firmly and with total conviction.

'Jak,' I said, 'you're crazy!'

He said nothing, and we leaned back again. I longed to see his face. The face of a real tout, right up close. I had only ever heard them whisper, at street corners and railway stations in all the cities of Europe, and I had always turned away with a sudden hot fear in my heart.

'Jak . . .' I started to say.

'*Please* send up a flare!' he whispered, beside himself.

'Jak,' I said, 'you'll curse me if I do that now. We've another four hours to go, d'you realize? And there'll be a ruckus, I know what to expect. Today's the twenty-first, and that's when they're issued schnapps over there, right now they've been given their schnapps with their rations, understand? And in half an hour they'll start shouting and singing and shooting, and maybe something really will happen. And when the Stukas come in the morning you'll be sweating with fear, they'll drop their bombs that close, and if I don't fire off a white flare we'll be mincemeat, and you'll curse me for sending up a flare now when nothing's happening. Believe me. Tell me some more about yourself. Where did you last do your – touting?'

He sighed deeply. 'In Cologne,' he said.

'At the main railway station?'

'No,' he went on listlessly, 'not always. Sometimes at the South station. It made more sense, you see, because the girls lived closer by. Lilli near the opera house, and Irma and Amadea off Barbarossa-Platz. You see,' his voice sounding weary as if he were falling asleep, 'sometimes when I'd snaffled a fellow at the main station he'd give me the slip on the way, and that was a nuisance; sometimes they got scared on the way or whatever, I don't know, and then they'd give me the slip, without saying a word. It was just too far, from the main station all the way there, and towards the end I often stood at the South station, because a lot of soldiers used to get out there thinking it was Cologne – I mean the main station. And from the South station it was only a stone's throw, it wasn't that easy to give me the slip. First' – now he leaned towards me – 'I always went to Amadea, she lived in a building that had a café, later it was destroyed by a fire bomb. Amadea, you know – she was the nicest. She paid me the most, but that wasn't why I went to her first, it really wasn't, you must believe me, truly it wasn't. Oh, you don't believe me, but that really wasn't why I went to her first, just because she paid the most, d'you believe me?' By now he was so intense that I simply had to say yes.

'But Amadea was often busy – funny, wasn't it? She was very often busy. She had a lot of regulars, and sometimes she'd walk the street, too, if business was slow. And when

Amadea was busy I was sad, so next I'd go to Lilli. Lilli wasn't bad either, but she drank, and women who drink are terrible, unpredictable, sometimes nasty, sometimes nice, but Lilli was still nicer than Irma. Irma, she was a cold fish, let me tell you. She'd pay ten per cent, and that was it. Ten per cent! There I'd often be running half an hour through the cold night, standing for hours at the station or sitting over some lousy beer in a bar, risking being picked up by the police, and then ten per cent! Shit, I tell you! So Irma was always my last choice. The next day, when I brought her the first customer, she'd give me the money. Sometimes only fifty pfennigs, and once only ten pfennigs – would you believe it? Ten pfennigs!'

'Ten pfennigs?' I asked, horrified.

'Yes,' he said. 'She'd only been paid one mark. That was all he had on him, the bastard.'

'A soldier?'

'No, a civilian, and a really old fellow at that. And she gave me hell as well! Oh, Amadea was different! She always paid me plenty. Never less than two marks. Even when she hadn't been paid anything. And then . . .'

'Jak,' I asked, 'sometimes she charged nothing?'

'That's right, sometimes she charged nothing. Just the opposite, I believe. She'd even give the soldiers cigarettes or sandwiches or just something extra.'

'Extra?'

'Yes. Extra. She was very generous. A very, very sad girl, I'm telling you. And she took a bit of an interest in me, too. Wanted to know where I lived and whether I needed any cigarettes and that kind of stuff. And she was pretty, I'd say the prettiest of the lot.'

I was about to ask what she looked like, but just at that moment the first Russian started yelling like a madman. A kind of howl went up, gathering other voices, and immediately the first shot was fired. I just managed to grab Jak by the edge of his greatcoat; with one leap he would have been over the top and away, straight into the arms of the Russians. They always run into the arms of the Russians, the fellows who clear out. I pulled the trembling figure back, very close to me. 'For God's sake be quiet! It's nothing. They're just a bit drunk, and then they yell and shout blindly over the parapet. And you have to keep your head down, because it's those shots that sometimes find their mark . . .'

Now we heard a woman's voice and, although we couldn't understand a word, we knew that they must have yelled and sung something very coarse. Her shrill laughter tore the night to shreds.

'Calm down,' I told the struggling, groaning boy, 'it won't last long, in a few minutes the commissar will notice and slap them about. They're not allowed to do that, and they're soon cured of what they're not allowed to do, just like us . . .'

But the yelling continued, and the wild shouting, and to make matters worse one of our own was firing from behind us. I clung to the boy, who was trying to push me away and clear out. From up ahead came yells, then a shout . . . then again yelling . . . shots, and once again the horrible voice of the drunk woman. Then total silence, a terrible silence . . .

'You see?' I said.

'Now – now they're coming . . .'

'No – just listen!'

We listened again, and there was nothing to be heard but the ghastly grinding of silence.

'Do be sensible,' I went on, wanting to hear at least my own voice. 'Didn't you see the muzzle flashes? They're at least two hundred yards away, and if they come you'll hear, you're bound to hear, I'm telling you.'

27

By this time he seemed to have ceased to care. He just sat there beside me, wordless, rigid.

'Tell me,' I asked, 'what did she look like, your Amadea?'

He seemed reluctant to answer. 'Pretty,' he said curtly, 'dark hair and shiny bright eyes, and she was very small, terribly small, you know?' He suddenly became talkative again: '. . . and a bit crazy. That's all you could call it. Every day she used a different name. Inge, Simone, Kathleen, whatever, almost every day a different one . . . or Susie Marie. She was a bit crazy, and often she wouldn't accept any money at all.'

I grabbed him by the arm. 'Jak,' I said, 'I'll send up a white flare now. I think I hear something.'

He held his breath. 'Yes,' he whispered, 'send up a flare, I can hear them, I'll go crazy if you don't . . .'

I held onto his arm, grabbed the loaded Very pistol, held it high over my head, and pulled the trigger. There was a whistling roar as if heralding the Last Judgment, and when the light spread out like a gentle, silver liquid – like shimmering Christmas lights – I had no time to look at his face, for I had heard nothing, nothing whatever, and had only sent up the flare in order to see his face, the face of a genuine tout. I had no time, for where that yelling had been before, that shrieking of a drunken woman, there was now a heaving mass of silent figures who ducked to the ground in the light and then suddenly came storming forward with their demented hurrahs. Nor did I have time to send up a red flare, for all around us the terrible furrow of war was opening up and burying us . . . I had to drag Jak out of the hole, and after I had somehow managed to pull him out and, screaming with fear, was bending over him to have at least a dying look at his face, he merely whispered, very softly: 'Want to have a good time, sir . . . ?' and I was brusquely hurled on top of him by a fierce, terrible hand.

But now my eyes saw nothing but blood, darker than the night, and the face of a crazy prostitute who had given herself for nothing and had even added a little something . . .

The Murder

'The old man's crazy,' I said in a low voice.

'More likely pissed, he's always pissed when he orders an attack. Take it from me, that's how it is.' I said nothing, and Heini's voice continued: 'He tanks up till he's deaf and blind, and then: Let's go! At 'em! To hell with that kind of courage . . . are you asleep?' His hand groped towards me, and he tugged at my belt.

'Stop it,' I said, slightly annoyed, 'I'm awake. But what I'd like to know is how to get out of this. I don't relish the idea of a hero's death – I can't really say why. And last time, I needn't tell you, we left fifteen men behind; we had to beat it, and the old man was hoarse with rage because he still had a sore throat . . .'

'Not a chance – ahead of us the Russians and behind us the Prussians, and us in the middle, on a very narrow black strip; all we can do is try and stay alive.'

Somewhere up front a flare shot into the sky, and a kind of pale shimmer flooded the bare, hilly ground . . .

'I'll be damned!' Heini suddenly cried, 'they're showing a light, those idiots – the shooting'll start any moment, you'll see.'

Behind us, where the command posts were located at the top of the slope, someone had apparently pulled away the blanket from a dug-out entrance, a bowed silhouette showed for a moment, then all was dark again; the flare had gone out too . . . as if its light had been swallowed up by the infinite darkness . . .

'That was the old man's hole, I hope they drop a load right in front of it, or right inside, then there'll be no attack tomorrow . . .'

We quickly ducked, for from somewhere ahead came the sound of a gentle crack, then there was a shattering explosion, and behind us on the hilltop a few low, blackish-red flames shot up from the earth. Then all was quiet again, and we listened intently for any noise or shouting to start up behind us. But the silence persisted . . .

'Seems they were lucky,' Heini muttered angrily. 'But it's the truth, isn't it – a nice direct hit on the old man's quarters, and tomorrow we'll have saved the lives of twenty men . . .'

We turned back to face the coal-black wall of the night.

'There he sits, the bastard, boozing away and mulling over his plan . . .'

'More likely asleep,' I said wearily.

'But he had a light!'

'He always has a light, even when he's asleep – I've been there a few times with dispatches. There were two candles burning, and he was asleep. His mouth open, snoring, probably pissed . . .'

'I see,' Heini said slowly, and something in that 'I see' made me take notice. I looked over to where he must be standing and listened to his breathing. 'I see,' he repeated, and I would have given a lot to be able to see his face: all I could make out, blacker than the black night, were the rough outlines of his figure, and suddenly I heard him start to clamber out of the hole. Small clods of earth trickled from the parapet, and I could hear his hands scrabbling for a grip at the top . . .

'What are you up to?' I asked nervously, scared to be alone in this hole.

'I've got to go, and in a hurry, I've got the shits, it may take a while.' He had reached the top, and soon I heard his footsteps disappearing off to the right before the darkness swallowed up all sound . . .

Alone now, I groped for the bottle of rot-gut and found it in the darkness right under the cold metal of the machine-gun case. I pulled out the stopper, wiped the lip of the bottle with my hand, and drank deeply. The first taste as it touched the roof of my mouth was horrible, but soon a comfortable warmth spread slowly through me. I drank again, and again; then once again, then huddled down onto the bottom of the hole, threw the blanket over me and lit my pipe. All fear had left me. I propped myself on one elbow, covered my face with my hands, leaving just enough room for my pipe, and dozed off . . .

I was woken by the weird clatter of the night plane, which concealed cunning and deadly accuracy behind its seeming decrepitude. We had every reason to fear it. I wondered where Heini was and turned round. I was met with an incredible sight: to the rear, along the top of the range of hills where the command posts were, I saw a large, bright spot in the night, an open dug-out entrance, and in the middle of that bright, wavering spot a candle flickering. Agitated voices of scurrying men came alive, the blanket was hastily pulled across, but it was too late: at that very moment the noise of the night plane's engine stopped for a fraction of a second, and just where the light had been a flame shot up that was instantly suffocated by the night. In the absolute silence one could sense everybody ducking, trembling as they flattened themselves on the ground. But the plane flew slowly on. Now from the slope came renewed shouts and the sounds of men digging: picks hacking into the stony soil, and beams were being dragged out . . .

At last Heini returned from over on the right; clambering

back into the hole he cursed: 'Goddammit, have I got the shits, I could've gone on for hours! Pass me the bottle, will you?'

His voice was quite calm, but when I passed him the bottle, waiting in the dark for his hand to touch mine so I would know he had hold of the bottle, I could feel him trembling violently. He drank long and deep, and I could hear him panting, and it seemed to me that the night had become even darker and more silent . . .

'By the way,' said Heini a little later, 'd'you know the old man is dead? Those were his quarters. Direct hit. I don't imagine he'll have felt a thing – after all, he was pissed . . .'

Vingt-et-Un

I drew an ace, gleefully placed my bet, drew a nine and said 'Pass.'

Fips turned up his card, a ten; then he smiled at me, for there were a hundred and twenty *pengö* in the kitty. Slowly he took the second card, a queen, then he drew a king and smiled again. And when he picked up the fourth card, I laughed . . . but he hadn't even looked at it when we suddenly flung ourselves to the ground: a strange, soft whirring sound was in the air. Our faces were deathly pale. Then from our right came an appalling crash, and immediately afterwards we heard a terrible scream, followed by nothing. There was total silence. Fips was still holding the fourth card face down as he looked at me: 'That was Alfred,' he said quietly, 'go and see what's happened to him.' There was still total silence, then we were startled again, this time by the shrill sound of the phone in the next dug-out. Fips jumped across me, threw the rest of the cards down onto the kitty, and flung aside the blanket. I could hear him answering the phone and saying 'Yes,' and again 'Yes,' and again, after a brief pause, a third time, 'Yes . . .'

He emerged, still holding the card. He looked stunned and absent-mindedly tucked the card under his corporal's shoulder strap. 'What was it?' I asked calmly.

'Christ!' he shouted at me. 'Aren't you going to go and find Alfred?' His eyes held a terrible fear, I forgave him for shouting at me, and I didn't dare ask him who it had been on the phone.

He walked the few steps to the edge of the forest with me and showed me the cable I had to follow to reach Alfred.

34

Alfred had gone off half an hour earlier to look for a break in the line. I glanced back into the trench and saw Fips standing there with that altogether strange, new fear in his face, saw him lean against the parapet and gaze out over the churned-up terrain. Then I picked up the cable and marched off into the unfamiliar undergrowth. I followed the trail that Alfred's feet had ploughed through the ferns; in some alarm I noticed that the path to the right was moving farther and farther out of sight and that the cable was leading me into totally unknown territory. It was so silent in the forest that my footsteps startled me, that soft, fluttery sound as I brushed against the fern fronds, the grazing of tendrils against my greatcoat, the soft swish of bobbing brambles . . .

Suddenly I felt the cable in my hands tightening; I pulled at it, but it didn't yield. Somewhere on the ground it must have been caught by a rock, a branch, or some heavy object. I pulled more vigorously and now discovered, just a few paces ahead of me, where it was pinned to the ground. Nervously I went closer, and then I saw him lying there, Alfred's grey figure, his face turned towards me. At the same moment I threw myself to the ground, for I suddenly saw that I was standing in a clearing that opened like a funnel into a hollow. I crawled slowly closer and first looked out across the dead man's body into that unfamiliar, shallow valley that was filled with an oppressive silence. Down there among the meadows flowed a little stream, and beyond it was a steep slope with a bare ridge.

Only then did I look at Alfred. His fixed eyes stared upwards, and involuntarily I followed his gaze into the mute green roof of beech leaves; at that moment I understood why he was smiling and lying there so calmly. His right hand still clasped the receiver of the testing set, and his

35

head was still tilted to the right in a listening pose. I carefully closed his eyelids and released his hand from the set; then, putting my arms round the dead man, I dragged him with me as I crawled slowly back into the forest . . .

It was as silent as it can only be in war. Those gentle, chirping sounds of a forest in summertime hummed around me; from somewhere up ahead I could hear the good-natured booming of a cannon, but the silence was stronger. I bent down, took Alfred's paybook from his breast pocket and, as I carefully leaned with my left hand on his chest, I heard a strange sound, almost like a sponge being squeezed. Alarmed, I pulled him up and discovered in his back a hole the size of a fist, its edges fringed with shreds of cloth. His whole back was sticky with blood. I lowered him again, removed the steel helmet from his head, and gazed silently at that childish forehead, at that childish mouth which only half an hour ago had laughingly placed his bet. Involuntarily and unknowingly, I called out in a loud, strained voice, 'Alfred, Alfred!' and it seemed to me that he must surely move, but my absorption was penetrated once again by the soft, cruel, menacing sound as of smouldering cotton wool . . . I threw myself down beside Alfred and this time heard the crash to my left, at the very spot where Fips must have stayed behind. Then all was silent again. I wrenched the testing set from Alfred's shoulder, connected it to the cable, and dialled. 'Cherry stone, switchboard,' a bored voice responded . . .

'Cherry stone three, please,' I said, and he repeated: 'Cherry stone three.' I heard him plug in and crank the handle; there followed that typical telephone exchange silence with only a few soft clicks audible. Again I heard him crank, then the voice said: 'Cherry stone doesn't answer.'

'Is there something wrong with the line?' I asked anxiously.

'No, the connection's all right, there seems to be nobody there.'

I hurriedly stuffed Alfred's paybook in my pocket, yanked the set free again and, following my own trail, ran back. After jumping into the trench I first listened for a moment but could hear nothing; then, crouching low, I ran along the trench until I saw Fips lying there . . .

There wasn't much left of him to recognize, his chest was ripped apart, and blood and bone splinters had swamped his face; only his shoulders were uninjured, and the card was still tucked under his left shoulder strap. I pulled it out: it was a king . . .

'Twenty-one,' I said softly, 'you win.' I walked back the few paces to where our kitty lay, picked up the notes, tore them into tiny pieces, and scattered the coloured scraps over him like flower petals.

At that moment the phone rang. I stepped across Fips's body into the dug-out, picked up the receiver, and answered. But there was nothing to be heard except for that typical telephone exchange silence and, obeying an obscure urge, I said 'Yes!' Now I understood the fear in Fips's eyes. Still no one responded, and again I said, in a loud, mocking voice: 'Yes!' And, following the rule of three, I repeated, now obedient and subdued: 'Yes.' Then I hung up, and I, too, went outside, leaned against the parapet, and waited . . .

Cause of Death: Hooked Nose

When Lieutenant Hegemüller returned to his billet, his thin face was trembling with a nervous pallor; his eyes seemed to have gone dead, his face under the flaxen hair was a blank, quivering surface. All day long he had been sitting in the communications room, relaying radio messages to the incessant accompaniment of the chatter of machine pistols as they spewed out their bullets over at the outskirts of the town into the wan afternoon light: over and over again that cackling screech of a new salvo, and knowing that every single link in that rattling chain of sound meant a destroyed or mutilated human life, a body writhing in the dust and tumbling down a slope! And every half hour, with hellish regularity, the thud of a muffled explosion, and knowing that that sound, fading like a retreating thunderstorm, replaced the work of gravediggers, gravedigging in the interests of sanitation; knowing that yet another section of the quarry was at that very moment collapsing over the harvest of the last half hour and burying the living with the dead . . .

For the thousandth time the lieutenant wiped his pale, sweat-soaked face; then with a curse he kicked open the door to his quarters and stumbled into his room, where with a groan he sat down on his chair. On and on and on rushed the venomous machinery of death – almost as if that ripping, crackling sound were the screech of a monstrous saw splitting the sky so it would collapse when the day's work was done. Often it seemed as though the traces of this destruction must be visible and, his face twitching, he would lean for a moment out of the window to see with his own eyes whether the vast grey vault of the sky were not already tilting like the prow of a foundering ship. He thought he could even hear the gurgling of the black water lying in wait to wash over the wreckage of the world and swallow it up in deadly calm.

Quaking in every limb, he smoked with trembling fingers, knowing that he must do something to fight this madness. For he felt that he was not without guilt, that he had been forced into the stony heart of guilt, a heart that must lie at the centre of this ceaselessly grinding atrocity. Neither the pain he suffered nor the nameless horror and mortal fear could wipe out the consciousness that *he* was shooting and *he* was being shot. Never before had he been so intensely aware of the great cosmic home that embraces all men, the reality of God.

On and on went that biting, grinding, spitting, demented sawing of the machine pistols. There followed a few minutes of a ghastly silence that must make the birds tremble in their hiding-places, and then a detonation: a charge of explosives, drilled into the wall of the quarry, replaced the grim labours of the gravediggers. And again shots, shots, one after the other in an endless chain, each one of them struck Lieutenant Hegemüller in his very heart.

But suddenly he heard a different sound, a subdued sound, the sobbing of a woman. He listened intently, rose to his feet and stepped out into the corridor, listened again for a moment, then flung open the kitchen door and stopped in his tracks: the Russian woman was on her knees, her fists covering her ears, and sobbing, sobbing so that the tears dripped from her blouse onto the floor.

For a moment the lieutenant was gripped by a strange, cold curiosity: tears, he thought, tears, never would I have believed a person could have so many tears. The pain was dripping in great, clear beads out of the elderly woman, collecting in a veritable puddle on the floor between her knees.

Before he had a chance to ask, the woman jumped up and screamed: 'They've taken him away, my Piotr, Piotr Stepanovich . . . oh sir, sir!'

'But he's not . . .' the lieutenant shouted back.

'No, sir, he's not a Jew, no. Oh sir, sir!'

The tears gushed from between the fingers that she was pressing against her face as if to staunch a bleeding wound . . .

Driven by some overpowering inner force, the lieutenant turned on his heel and, calling out something to the woman, dashed out into the street.

The streets were completely deserted. An eerie tension hung in the air: what hovered over the little town was not only the terror of those crouching in their hiding-places, not only the whip of death. The silence, which filled the streets like pale, grey dust, held a kind of mockery as if one devil were grinning at another.

The lieutenant raced along, sweat dripping from every pore, the terrible sweat that was no release but more like a death sweat poisoned by a bestiality that had been saturated with the killers' vicious lust. A strange burning cold flowed over him from the dead façades of the houses. And yet he was filled with something like joy – no, it actually was joy – what a glorious feeling to run for the life of a human being! In those minutes, racing through the streets at breakneck speed, almost beside himself, his subconscious came to understand many things; a thousand things were revealed to him from out of that nebulous haze he had called his ideology, rising like stars to pierce him with their brilliance and then die away like comets, but their reflection remained within him, as an accumulated source of subdued light.

Panting, covered with dust, he reached the outskirts of the town where the doomed had been herded together at the edge of the steppe. They formed a square surrounded by vehicles mounted with machine guns; in the vehicles, guards lounged behind the slim barrels, smoking their cigarettes.

At first Hegemüller ignored the sentry who tried to stop him, did not react when the man grabbed him by the sleeve. For a second he stared into the man's face, amazed at how close and clear it was. In fact, the faces of the sentry cordon seemed all equally dull-witted and brutish whereas the faces of those inside the cordon seemed in some exquisite manner to have been lifted high above the mass and placed on the pinnacle of humanity. A sombre silence hung over the crowd, something strangely vibrating, flut-tering, like the flapping of heavy banners, something solemn, and – Hegemüller felt, as his heart missed a beat – inexplicably comforting, joyful; he felt this joy surge through him, and at that instant he envied the doomed people and was shocked to realize that he was wearing the same uniform as the murderers. Blushing with shame he turned towards the sentry and croaked: 'The man whose house I'm billeted in is here. He's not a Jew . . .' and since the sentry stood there in apathetic silence he added: 'Grimschenko, Piotr . . .'

An officer approached the group and raised his eyebrows at the sight of the dusty, sweat-soaked lieutenant, who was wearing neither belt nor cap. Hegemüller now realized that the executioners and their minions were all drunk. With their bloodshot eyes they looked like bulls, and their breath was like steam from a manure heap. Once again Hegemüller stammered out the name of his host, and the lieutenant in command of the minions scratched his head in a display of gruesome good nature and asked lamely: 'Innocent, you mean?'

'Innocent, that too,' Hegemüller replied curtly.

The lieutenant seemed taken aback as this little word fell into the pool of his heart. But the word had sunk without trace, without raising ripples, as the lieutenant stepped in front of the doomed figures and shouted: 'Grimschenko, Piotr, step forward!' Since nobody moved, and that strangely fluttering silence persisted, he called out the name again, adding: 'Can go home!' And when there was still no response he stepped back and said awkwardly: 'Gone, maybe already done for, maybe still over there – come with me!'

Hegemüller's eyes followed the finger pointing towards the place of execution.

What he saw was the edge of an enormous quarry that sloped towards the assembly point, and a row of close-ranked soldiers armed with machine pistols. From the assembly point, a procession of the doomed led up to the rim of the quarry, where it flattened out: from this rim the regular, whiplike cracking of the machine pistols sounded through the afternoon air.

And once again, as he followed the drunken lieutenant, it seemed to Hegemüller that the crowd, the doomed crowd, had dissolved into a procession of noble personalities, while the few murderers seemed like brutish clods. Each one of those faces he so anxiously scanned in search of Grimschenko seemed to him calmer, revealing an inexpressibly human gravity. The women with babies in their arms, old people and children, men, girls smeared with faeces who had apparently been pulled out of latrines for the purpose of being murdered; rich and poor, ragged and well-dressed, all were endowed with a sublimity that left Hegemüller speechless. The lieutenant tried to make conversation by throwing out oddly apologetic fragments, not as an excuse for the killings but to gloss over his drunken condition while on duty: 'Tough job, this, you know. Couldn't stand it without booze . . . hope you understand . . .'

But Hegemüller, in whom horror had aroused a strange and sober calm, was nagged by a single question: What do they do with the babies, the tiny ones who can't stand or walk – how is it technically possible? Meanwhile his eyes never left the procession of the doomed, never rose to the rim of the quarry where the pallid afternoon was punctured by the thwacking and spitting of the machine pistols. But on reaching the point where the slope flattened out and he was forced to lift his gaze, he saw the answer to that nagging question. He saw a black boot kicking the bloodied corpse of an infant into the abyss and, averting his eyes in horror and looking along the rim of the quarry, he suddenly saw Grimschenko at the head of the line, saw him collapse under a bullet. With a wild and terrible cry he shouted 'Stop, stop!' so loud that the executioners held their fire in alarm. He seized the lieutenant by the arm and dragged him over to where Grimschenko, drenched in blood, was hanging half over the edge. He had not tipped forward into the quarry but, facing away from his killer, had fallen over backwards.

Hegemüller grabbed him and lifted him up, and just then an official voice shouted from somewhere: 'Everyone get back – blasting!' Hegemüller did not see the killers running back fifty yards in their panic, or the astonished, bewildered face of the lieutenant in charge of his drunken minions.

Hegemüller had grasped Grimschenko's body and hoisted him onto his shoulders; he could feel the flowing blood congealing between his fingers. Behind him the detonation exploded in a cloud of leaden sound into the sky; scarcely a foot or two behind Hegemüller, the rim of the quarry collapsed, and the earth buried both the dead and the half-dead, the infants and the old men who for ninety-four years had borne the burden of life . . .

It was no surprise to Hegemüller that the row of killers, waiting with smoking barrels and dull eyes for the next batch, made way for him without resistance. He felt he had the power to force them all onto their knees with a single glance, a single word, those butchers of men in their brand-new uniforms, for in the midst of the red fog of confusion, fear and noise, of stench and anguish, he had felt something that filled him with happiness: Grimschenko's gentle breath that brushed his shoulder like a caress from another world, that tiny breath of the gravely wounded, whose blood had caked his fingers.

Unhindered he passed through the row of murderers, hearing behind him the upsurge of renewed firing. He found a waiting vehicle and shouted at the dozing driver: 'Get going – the nearest field hospital!' as he jerked open the door, let Grimschenko slide from his shoulders, and laid him on the back seat.

Suddenly he was dreaming: he was running, running, with a number of others in a mad, gruelling race to a lake in whose waters they wanted to cool off. The heat burned over them, and all round them. The whole world was one pitiless furnace, and they ran and ran, while the sweat flowed from their pores like streams of sour blood. It was an indescribable torture, this race along a dusty road to the lake which they knew lay beyond a curve in the road, yet it was a sensual pleasure, this sweating, a kind of swimming in torture, a dreadful yet in some mysterious way pleasurable torture, while the sweat flowed, flowed, flowed. And then came that curve in the road beyond which must be the lake; with a wild cry he raced round the curve, saw the glittering silver surface of the water, plunged into it with a jubilant shout, knelt down and joyfully dipped his face in the water. Then, just as he was marvelling at how miraculously cool the water was despite the scorching heat, he woke up and opened his eyes.

He was looking into the impassive face of an orderly who was holding an empty jug, and he instantly grasped that he had fainted and been revived with a dash of cold water. He could smell some kind of disinfectant, could hear a typewriter tapping. 'Grish, Grimschenko?' he whispered, but the orderly, instead of replying, turned away. 'So the Russian's name is Grimschenko – now you can complete the medical report, Sister.'

The orderly stepped aside, and Hegemüller felt the cool professional hand of a doctor on his forehead and heard a complacent voice say: 'Been overdoing it a bit, eh?' Then the hand slid down his sleeve to his pulse and, while Hegemüller was feeling his own pulse beating irregularly against the doctor's gentle fingers, the complacent voice spoke again: 'All right, Sister – got it? Then write down: Cause of death – let's say, hooked nose,' and then the complacent voice laughed while the hands belonging to that complacent voice were feeling Hegemüller's pulse almost tenderly. But Hegemüller sat up, took in the white room with a strangely detached expression, then laughed too, and his laughter was as strange as his expression. His eyeballs rolled back as his laughter grew louder and louder; they dimmed and seemed to turn ever further inward, like the closing shutters

45

of a searchlight, taking the whole world inside with them and leaving nothing but a clouded emptiness; Hegemüller laughed, and from then on the only words he ever spoke were: 'Cause of death: hooked nose.'

Vive la France!

The sentry groped his way across the dark room to the door, opened it and stepped out into the corridor; for half a second he hesitated in the doorway, reluctant to leave the warmth of the room behind him and go out into the cold night. He slowly closed the door and merged with the darkness of the corridor. He could see nothing, he was merely aware that the front door was open, and subconsciously he was surprised to find that the cold which had greeted him in the corridor seemed to be intensified outside: damp, icy, remorseless, it advanced upon him through the open doorway. Then, standing in the entrance, completely enveloped by that damp cold, he was able to distinguish, more or less from memory, the vague outlines of the trees in the park, the furrow of the avenue, on the right the ruined factory whose sinister black wall seemed to rise like a barrier between two underworlds . . .

A weary, almost desperate voice called out: 'Is that you?'

'Yes,' he replied, surprised to find he had the strength to utter that one syllable. A deathly fatigue flowed like lead through his limbs, as if dragging him down; his eyelids drooped, and leaning against the front door he fell into a sleep that lasted perhaps for a second, a voluptuous, heavy stupor. To sleep, ah, to sleep.

The sentry he was relieving bumped into him; with a sense of searing pain he was awake again. 'It's all yours,' said the voice, a voice that contained something like pity.

He couldn't even summon the strength to ask for a cigarette, to open his mouth at all. He was paralyzed by the hopeless deathly fatigue which was suffocating him. His eyes burned like hot coals in their sockets, from his empty stomach rose a sourish, nauseating fluid; his arms and legs were like lumps, numb, leaden. Without knowing it, he uttered muffled, brutish sounds as he collapsed onto stone slabs. But he couldn't sleep: it wasn't the cold that prevented him – he had slept under more difficult conditions and in worse cold – no, he was overstimulated by fatigue. So there he remained, squatting on his heels, wrapped in cold and night, at the top of the wide flight of stone steps – a bundle of misery, with two hours ahead of him, a mountain of agonizing eternity.

Suddenly he realized from the sounds coming from the upper floor of the château that the festivities were not yet over. Laughter, subdued voices, reached him, partly through the corridor, partly through the thickly curtained window. And now something awoke in him, tiny at first yet strong, a raging, minute inner chill, a crystalline chill mounting inside him like a surging spring that froze instantly but continued to grow, a column of ice, rising layer upon layer, and by which he pulled himself up: HATRED. Lost in thought he straightened up, leaned against the wall, and smoked. His fatigue was still there, as well as that nauseating, sour malaise; but now hatred had reared up like a column to support him.

Immediately above his head the door to the little balcony suddenly opened. A lurid light flooded the garden, and the next moment he recognized the conceited voice of the captain; at the same time, someone was pissing from the balcony down onto the steps. He jumped aside in alarm.

Then it was as if the light were being sucked back out of the garden, swallowed up, while the shadows of the two door panels widened; and, just before the last of the light was shut in, he heard that conceited voice saying: 'Let's call it a day, gentlemen, it's two o'clock . . .'

The smell from the puddle on the steps drove him into the garden. With heavy legs, his hands clasped behind him, he plodded as far as the corner of the building.

Then the strident voice of the drunken lieutenant shouted in the corridor 'Vive la France!' and burst into peals of laughter over his own wit. In the dimly luminous night the sentry saw the lieutenant staggering down the steps. He remained quite still while with the frantic assurance of the drunk the figure stumbled through the garden parallel to the building, then took the bend too sharply and pitched forward towards the corner.

'What the devil are you doing here?' came the lieutenant's shaky voice.

The sentry's silence hung menacingly in the air. Like a hunter, as he leaned calmly against the wall, he watched the swaying figure as it thrust its corrupted child's face with its torrid breath close to his.

'Can't you hear me? Aren't you at least going to challenge me?'

'Yessir,' the sentry replied stoutly.

'And I'm telling you, shoot down anyone who doesn't know the password – anyone, without mercy.'

And as if obsessed with that idea, he repeated stubbornly: 'Shoot to kill! Shoot to kill!' Without waiting for the sentry's reply, he staggered towards the gate, out into the avenue and, just before turning left into the silent village street, shouted once again: 'Vive la France!' His hysterical laughter bounced off the walls of the houses into the park.

With short, quick steps the sentry walked as far as the gate and looked out into the village street; there stood the houses black and silent, and above the outline of their roofs the darkness softened to a watery ink. He could hear the lieutenant's footsteps, hear him kick a stone on the road, follow him in his mind's eye as he turned right into the church square, and could hear muffled knocking on a door. The sentry nodded as if in confirmation when the lieutenant's hoarse, childish voice called out reproachfully, 'Yvette! Yvette!'

The church square, opening out to the right beyond the corner, formed an oblique angle with the village street, so that with his last thirty paces the lieutenant had come closer to the sentry again and was standing half-turned towards him. His voice now reached the sentry over the low, dark houses. There was something eerie in the way it seemed to float over the one-storey buildings, always repeating the same words, first reproachfully, 'Yvette, Yvette!', then impatiently, in a childish whine, 'Open up!' And again reproachfully, 'Yvette, damn you!' Next came a strange silence, and the sentry, listening with bated breath, could visualize the door opening soundlessly and white arms pulling the lieutenant inside. But breaking the paralyzing silence the lieutenant suddenly cried out in a shrill voice, 'Yvette, you bitch!' Then apparently the door really did open, there was the sound of throaty laughter, and the sentry, standing there in the cold night with eyes closed, his face screwed up with pain, saw quite clearly: the soothing smile on the white face of the girl.

Although he loved neither Yvette nor the lieutenant, he was seized, as he stood shivering beside the gatepost, by an agonizing jealousy, a fierce sense of total desolation, overshadowing even his hatred.

While he tensed to catch every sound, his fatigue had almost evaporated; he turned right and walked down the village street. Since he could never see more than a few paces ahead, the night seemed to be forever retreating. Each step seemed to bring him closer to the dark, black wall that blocked his view; a cruel game, it seemed to him, because even so the distance never diminished. And as a result of this game, the village, that wretched little place of twenty-three houses, a factory, and two run-down châteaux, became boundless, and it seemed an age before he reached the iron fence surrounding the school playground. From the kitchen the smell of stale, watery soup penetrated all the way to the street. Leaning over the low wall that supported the fence he called in a clear, subdued voice, 'Hullo there, Willi!'

He heard footsteps coming from the direction of the kitchen; then a dark figure loomed into view. 'Here,' the sentry called, 'I'm over here!' Looking half-asleep, Willi approached the fence, walked along beside it, and stepped through the gate into the street.

'What time is it?'

Willi clumsily rolled up his tunic, fumbled for his watch, pulled it out, and held it close to his face: 'Ten past two.'

'That's impossible – your watch must have stopped – no, no, that can't be right!'

His voice was trembling dangerously; the sentry waited breathlessly while Willi held the watch to his ear, shook it, then looked at its face again.

'It's going all right, I knew it was, my watch has never stopped yet.'

His voice showed no emotion. The sentry stood there without a word; his face was screwed up and withdrawn, hard and tormented.

'Oh, shut up,' said Willi, although the sentry hadn't said anything. 'Why must you always be so childish? Two hours are two hours, there's nothing you can do about it.'

The sentry stood there like a pillar of salt. Ten minutes! he kept thinking, and this single thought pounded away in his brain. Ten minutes, twelve times ten minutes, a hundred and twenty times one minute!

'Look,' Willi went on in a complacent tone, 'I always think of home, that passes the time for me. One day the war will be over, then we'll go back, take off our tunics, kiss our wives, and go off to work. We've done our duty, see? And we . . .'

'Shut up!'

The two men looked at each other with hostility, although all they could see of each other was a pale, blurred disc under the black shadow of the steel helmet. Yet each saw the other's face quite plainly, forming it from the sound of the voice and the tension in the air. Willi saw a thin, dark, bitter face with lacklustre eyes, shadowed by grief: the sentry's face. He in turn saw that good-natured, rather cunning, smug face, a bit surprised yet watchful; Willi's face.

'Give me a cigarette,' the sentry croaked.

'Hey, listen, you already owe me three. Tell you what, let's make that deal with the watch. For God's sake, a broken watch, what good is it to you! I'll give you twenty-five for it, ten now, that makes thirteen, and the rest the day after tomorrow when the canteen opens – I needn't tell you . . .'

'Shut up, just hand them over!'

Willi hesitated for a moment, then put his hand in his pocket and pulled out a packet of cigarettes.

'Here – but where . . .'

The sentry snatched the packet from Willi, opened it, and instantly struck a match. Suddenly the two faces were harshly lit up and looked frighteningly similar: pale, unspeakably weary, slack-mouthed.

'Are you crazy, man?' exclaimed Willi, 'and then . . .'

'Oh, shut up.' The sentry's voice now sounded more conciliatory. 'They can lick my . . .'

At that he turned on his heel but swung round again and asked: 'What time is it now?'

Again Willi carefully rolled up his tunic, groped for his watch in the little pocket in his waistband, and held it up to his eyes: 'Eighteen minutes past – don't forget the watch!'

The sentry strolled down the street as far as the second house and leaned against the door of Madame Sevry's café. He drew deeply and voluptuously on his cigarette, and an extraordinary happiness filled his entire being. The poison radiated a gentle, pleasant vertigo. He closed his eyes. Ten cigarettes, he thought. Now he actually began to feel time slipping between his fingers; that heavy, black, inert, remorseless lump was melting away. It was as if a floodgate had opened and the current was bearing him away.

On either side the road led off into the abyss of darkness; now the silence was released, it too was flowing. For eighteen endless minutes the silence had been like a brake holding back time. Now the silence ran parallel with time, so close to it that the two seemed to be one.

Knowing just where the château was on the right and the school on the left, he imagined he could see them. But the avenue leading from the road to the château – that he really could see. It was like a high, perforated wall, darker than the night and studded with the dim clarity of the sky.

When he carefully tucked away the stub of his cigarette in his pocket, he knew that no more than seven minutes had passed. So it must be twenty-five past two. He decided to take a walk through the factory, that would take care of twelve minutes, and after that to smoke a cigarette. If he then returned slowly to Madame Sevry's door, smoked another cigarette, and walked to the school, it would have to be three o'clock.

Moving away from the door he walked down the gentle slope to the château gates, then slowly on almost to the corner of the church square – sixty-seven paces – where he turned left towards the abandoned gatehouse. From the archway he glanced into the little house from which all the timberwork had been stolen. As he hurried on he suddenly realized he was scared. Yes, without rhyme or reason, he was scared. Who could possibly be looking for anything in this completely looted factory at two thirty in the morning? But he was scared. His footsteps resounded hollowly on the concrete floor, and through the damaged roof he could see scraps of blue-black sky. It seemed to him as if the bare, black room were soaking up the threats of silence through the holes in the roof. The factory had been so radically gutted that it was no longer possible to make out what it had been used for: a big, bare hall where the concrete bases of the machines seemed glued stubbornly to the floor; meaningless iron structures, dirt, torn paper: indescribably cold and dreary.

Rigid with fear, the sentry walked slowly to the end of the great hall where an open doorway led outside. In the blackness of the wall, the open doorway looked like a rectangular piece of dark grey-blue cloth. He headed straight for it, walking softly, for the sound of his footsteps frightened him. Suddenly he stumbled over the rails leading outside, caught himself as he staggered against the wall, and stood with a pounding heart in the doorway. Although here, too, he could see scarcely twenty paces ahead, he believed he must be looking at the wide, open field, for he knew it was there and he could smell it: the sharp sweetness of spring nights above the meadows and fields.

54

Suddenly his fear flared up and landed right in the middle of his heart. Trembling, he turned round and walked with hesitant steps into the soundless menace, and the farther he went the more he realized that it – his fear – was empty, hollow, and he began to feel almost light-hearted. He even smiled a little as he stepped through the narrow doorway in the black wall into the grounds of the château.

It was like a dream! This round he had made seemed to have taken so long, an entire lifetime, as he mounted the stone stairs again, stepped across the captain's puddle, and stationed himself in the entrance. It was an eerie feeling: time seemed to have passed with ghostly speed yet insane sluggishness, time was disembodied, intangible, contradictory. How terrible to be at its mercy – it was a dream!

The only realities were the puddle, the cold, and the damp. He decided against walking round the château and proceeded to light a cigarette. His calculations became confused, he had merely a dim notion: one cigarette here and one in Madame Sevry's doorway, then off to Willi, and it would have to be three o'clock. So one hour would have passed. He knew he was deceiving himself, yet, while aware of that, he believed in the deception.

How am I going to tell Willi that I don't even have the watch any more, he thought in desperation, that two evenings ago I drank it away at Madame Sevry's! I have to hold him off till the day after tomorrow and then return the cigarettes to him out of my canteen rations. Franz will have to get twelve, Willi thirteen, so all I'll have left will be seven cigarettes and the tobacco.

And the money he had borrowed! Credit is the worst of all traps for a poor man, he thought bitterly. It was always the same: whenever Marianne's parcels arrived with the money she sent, he would blow it all, it would run through his fingers; after that he would drag himself along over the perilous, seductive bridge of credit, swaying between the abysses of despair and stupor.

And the war stood still! That monster was marking time. Horror without end. Day and night the uniform, and the futility of routine duty, the arrogant, strident bad temper of the officers and the yelling of the NCOs. They had been driven into the war like a hopeless, vast, grey herd of desperate men. Sometimes the memory of the front, where the monster really had been bare-fanged and bloody, seemed to him easier to endure than the perpetual waiting in this country that vacillated between spiteful muteness and a kindly, gentle irony. Again and again, on the monotonous carousel of the so-called deployment plan, they were shoved for a short time into the dug-outs and then back into this lousy dump, where they knew every single child, every chair and every bar. And the wine was getting worse and worse, the schnapps ever more dubious, cigarettes and rations ever scarcer; it was a cruel game. He tucked the second butt into his little watch pocket, stepped unconcernedly into the captain's puddle, and walked rapidly down the avenue, towards the street, straight to the school.

Good as his word, Willi was standing by the entrance to the building, apparently gently dozing.

'What time is it?' asked the sentry in a hectoring tone. He waited impatiently while Willi completed his fumbling manoeuvre with the watch.

'Quarter to,' Willi answered. 'Did you bring it along?'

'Bring what along?'

'The watch. You could've just gone to your room to pick it up, couldn't you? I want to send home a parcel tomorrow morning, you see, and . . .'

'I left it with the watchmaker in Bechencourt – didn't I tell you? It'll be Monday before I can give it to you.'

'Oh, you might've told me. So I s'pose I'll have to pay for the repair, won't I?'

The sentry laughed. 'Of course, then you'll have a good watch for twenty-five cigarettes and a few francs – cheap, eh?'

'But we made a deal, and – and are you sure, Monday? Or d'you think . . . ?'

'No, Monday for sure.'

The sentry was obsessed with the single thought that it was only a quarter to three. Not even an hour, not even half the time, had gone by! A profound bitterness welled up in him, hatred and rage, a dark fear and, at the same time, despair. All this seemed to choke him, his throat felt bitter and hot and horribly dry, as if from violently suppressed tears.

'Be seeing you,' he said in a forced voice as he turned away. He was about to ask the time again, but it was so pointless, it couldn't possibly be more than ten minutes to three.

The street, which he walked along so often during the day and again in the evening to fetch rations – during the day this little bit of street seemed absurdly short and pitiful; now at night it had acquired a mysterious length and breadth. Even the dirty, shabby houses opposite the château grounds were more impressive in the dark. But all he could feel was that desperate bitterness that was almost strangling him. Not even the thought of the cigarettes in his pocket was any comfort, nor was the knowledge that the awkward business of the watch had been postponed for at least two days. He was miserably cold and hungry – a naked, nagging hunger. He put his hands in his pockets, but they were so

57

hopelessly numb that even in there they refused to come to life. His steel helmet suddenly weighed on him like a lump of lead, and at that moment he felt convinced that everything, everything, hatred and torment and despair, was contained in that steel helmet, in that heavy lump on his forehead. He took it off, then stepped into Monsieur Dubuc's gateway, just opposite the entrance to the château.

Now that he was rid of the pressure of the helmet he felt almost light-headed, and unconsciously he was smiling, a gentle, benign smile. He thought: now it *must* be three o'clock! And once the first half had gone by, time passed more quickly: the half-way mark was the ridge that had to be climbed, after that it was downhill all the way. He pictured Marianne's face while closing his eyes, making it appear so close and vivid that he could smell her hair. There would be some mail from her again, he would see her handwriting . . .

Time flowed, flowed, he could sense it, at breakneck speed it was approaching four o'clock. To sleep, to sleep and dream till six! The thought of tomorrow's duty checked him for a moment like a horse at a hurdle, but then, suddenly, for the first time that night, he heard the striking of the village clock: four strokes and three strokes, relentlessly. Three o'clock! Only three o'clock!

The shock made him duck like a beaten animal; he cringed as if from a cruel blow, gave a groan of animal despair, tried without conviction to kid himself that he'd miscounted. His bare head suddenly felt ice-cold and painful. He jammed on his steel helmet, lit a cigarette, and in feverish haste, inhaling deeply, smoked two cigarettes, one after another, slavering with hatred, rage and despair.

He even forgot to save up the two butts, flicking them brusquely into the street . . .

After that, when he walked across to Willi it was eight minutes past three; the next time – it seemed like an eternity of inner torment – it was eleven minutes past three. Those three minutes had been an eternity! Yes, he was done for, that was it; it was all futile. It would never be four o'clock, he would never reach the fourth hour alive, he would be crushed by the hideous millstones of naked time. All comfort and hope had sunk out of sight; not even memory could conjure them up now. There remained nothing but the naked torture of time and the prospect of going on four hours' duty the next day, suffering from hunger and lack of sleep, with the hung-over lieutenant. Rifle drill, about-turn, rifle drill, about-turn, field training, rifle drill, target practice, singing, singing, singing! Four hours: an endless chain of murderous seconds. Four hours! And these two were not even over yet. Time was a cheat, that was it! It cheated him, it destroyed every hope. Two hours! Four hours! Parade-ground duty and sentry duty, hopelessly clamped in this vice! Singing! Singing! Singing songs to satisfy the hung-over lieutenant's sentimental nature.

From the knotted tangle of rage, despair and hatred, hatred now emerged isolated and pure. He embraced that hatred and nursed it; he nurtured it with spiteful phrases about the lieutenant, the pissing captain, and the NCOs. With a ghastly smile he lit his fifth cigarette, standing once again in Madame Sevry's doorway, and looked along the street.

Now he could release that hatred, he no longer needed to nurse and nurture it; it was strong enough to work away independently inside him.

From the sea came a faint wind, damp and cool, that prompted unusual sounds: the groaning of fresh-leaved

59

trees, the creaking of rotting roof-timbers, and the rattle of
old, warped doors.

And all at once he knew that time really had passed swiftly;
he was not surprised to hear the clock strike a quarter to four.

He hurried back through the avenue and entered the
guard-room to rouse his relief. Waking a man is an art, he
thought, a soldier's sleep is something sacred, which is why
it is kicked around by everyone: hardly anyone knows how to
rouse a soldier from his sleep, the sleep that costs nothing but
is so indescribably precious.

He groped his way across the room and cautiously woke
the sentry, not too tentatively and not too brutally – in such a
way that the man was immediately awake yet not torn
ruthlessly from the profound bliss of sleep. He shook the
sentry a few times gently but firmly, and a resigned voice
mumbled, 'All right, I'm coming.'

Pity overwhelmed him; they were all, all of them, clamped
into this senseless, cruel system. He waited outside at the
entrance to the avenue; he no longer felt cold or hungry,
hardly even tired, now that he was sure of his bed.

But suddenly he heard footsteps coming from the church
square, strange footsteps, groans, and little yelps of suppressed lust. The staggering was so palpable in the darkness that
he could picture the lieutenant, weaving from side to side,
sometimes walking briskly, then lurching again. Yvette must
have regaled him nicely with her phony liqueurs! Now he
was turning into the village street . . . For ten paces the
lieutenant walked almost normally, humming to himself,
then staggered again; and then – then the sentry saw the
glowing tip of his cigarette.

Shoot him, shoot him! he thought, and scarcely had the
words entered his mind than he released the safety catch of
his rifle and aimed it, leaning his left hand on the gatepost

and pushing the barrel across it. He was ice-cold and alert, tense with the glorious game of aiming at the lieutenant. And after taking precise aim at the glowing cigarette, he called, keeping his voice down: 'Password – who goes there?' He followed the approaching figure with his rifle, and when the voice called back 'Vive la France!' he was transfixed by a terrible, savage emotion known only to gamblers who suddenly and compulsively bet everything on a single card: he pressed the trigger. And in the billionth of a second between pressure and discharge, everything within him that was still human, all of it, longed for the bullet to miss, but a sickening, brief, gurgling sound told him otherwise. He was standing there rigid and motionless when the relief sentry grabbed his arm and asked in a scared voice, 'What happened?'

'Vive la France,' he merely replied and, with chalk-white face and trembling hands, leaned his rifle against the gatepost.

The Casualty

At the point where, half an hour earlier, the dust cloud of
the attackers had been, there was now the dust cloud of
fleeing men. The dusty haze was drifting over the shimmering steppe towards the military police, confusing them and
increasing their fury. Raising their machine pistols they
roared: 'Stop, you bastards – stop – back to your positions!'

The air was filled with the screams of wounded men left
lying on the ground, the shouts of the Russians – a hoarse,
frightened barking, and the cries of fleeing men: like a herd
of wild horses scenting an obstruction, they halted when
confronted by the barrels of the machine pistols, then
turned in weary submission and went back.

From behind me I could hear the shouts of the officers as
they grouped their men for a new thrust. I could hear the
rumbling of tanks, the howling of shells, and still the
screams of the badly wounded. Slowly and with a feeling of
extraordinary happiness I walked towards the line of
military police. They couldn't touch me, I'd been wounded,
although there was nothing to show for it in front.

'Stop!' they shouted. 'Get back there, you bastard!'

'I've been wounded!' I yelled at them. With suspicious
looks they let me approach. I went up to a tense, infuriated
lieutenant, turned round and showed him my back. It must
have been a pretty big hole, I'd run my hand over it once:
damp, sticky blood and shreds of cloth. But I could feel
nothing, it was a superb wound, a wound made to order,
they couldn't touch me. Actually it must have looked worse
than it was. The lieutenant growled something, then said
more calmly: 'There's a doctor over there.'

The valley was empty and silent: half an hour earlier it had contained tanks, artillery, staff officers in their vehicles, the whole hysterical uproar that precedes an attack. Now it was quiet. The doctor was sitting under a tree. Behind me, more wounded men were slowly arriving. I was the first patient of this attack.

'Over here, my friend,' said the doctor. He lifted the shreds of cloth. It tickled a bit; then he clucked his tongue and said: 'Spit, please.' I gagged, my throat was all dry, but I managed to produce a blob.

'Nothing,' said the doctor. 'You've been lucky, doesn't seem to be anything in your lungs. But, Jesus, that could've been a bad one!' He gave me a tetanus shot. I asked for some water, and he pulled out a flask. I reached out for it, but he held it to my mouth and allowed me only a brief swallow. 'Take it easy, lad – d'you have any pain?'

'Yes.'

He gave me a pill. I swallowed it. I didn't feel a thing, it was a marvellous wound, made to order, it would take at least four months for the hole to heal, and by that time the war would be over.

'There, you can go now,' said the doctor. Next in line stood a man who had been shot in the calf; he was groaning with pain, but he had walked all the way here, using his rifle as a stick.

The valley was magnificent, the loveliest valley I had ever seen. Just bare slopes covered with steppe grass sweltering in the sun. A hazy sky above, nothing else. But it was the most magnificent valley, as glorious as my wound that didn't hurt me and yet was serious. I walked slowly, no longer thirsty and with no back-pack – I'd left that at the front. And I was alone. I sat down somewhere and had a smoke. All this takes time off the war, I thought, they can't

touch you, you've been wounded and you're entitled to a bit
of a rest. From my vantage point I could look down on the
place where the doctor was. There were a lot of men down
there, some of them walking along the valley and looking in
that barren scene like strollers in the desert. A car was parked
there too, right beside the doctor, but I didn't feel like being
driven in it, I had plenty of time, they couldn't touch me.

Slowly I walked on. Only now did I realize what a long way
we had advanced from Jassy. No matter how often I reached
the top of a ridge, there was nothing of the town's white walls
to be seen. It was very quiet, apart from a few desultory shots
in the distance. Then I saw a forest, and out of the forest came
a big, furious car raising a cloud of dust. It was really angry,
that car, impatient, irritable, annoyed. It stopped right in
front of me. In it sat our general, wearing his steel helmet,
and when generals wear their steel helmets something has
gone wrong. There was also a colonel, wearing a Knight's
Cross, no other decoration. It looked very chic and elegant.
The general stood up in the car and yelled at me: 'What d'you
suppose you're doing?'

'I've been wounded, sir,' I replied, and turned round. I
almost had to laugh, it was so funny the way I turned my
backside to the general.

'It's all right, son.' I turned again. His round, red face was
still furious, as furious as the car, even though he'd said 'son'.
Generals always say 'son'; they don't show much imagination when they speak to you.

'How are things up front?' he asked.

'First they went back, then forward again, I don't really
know.'

'Where's your rifle, son?'

'Smashed, sir. It was a hand grenade, fell right beside me.
My rifle lay on that side and got smashed to pieces.'

64

'Here, have a smoke,' he said, handing me a whole packet of cigarettes. Generals usually hand out cigarettes. I thanked him by standing to attention, and off they drove. The colonel touched his cap, which I found quite something considering he had the Knight's Cross and I had nothing on my chest.

On coming out of the forest I saw the town lying all white on its hills and looking magnificent. I felt very happy, they couldn't touch me, I'd been wounded right at the front, ten metres away from the Russians, and maybe I was a hero. They couldn't touch me. I was carrying my haversack, it contained two pairs of socks, and for that I would drink some wine in town, maybe get something to eat, but the idea of eating made me feel quite sick; I'd had nothing to eat or drink for a day and a half. Yet at the thought of the wine I walked faster. I crossed a heath that was all torn up by tank tracks and bombs; a few corpses were lying around, and some dead horses. Beyond this bit of heath the path rose steeply past some houses: I was in town. A tram was waiting in a square. I ran to catch it, like at home. I just made it, and we moved off at once. Maybe the driver had seen me, I thought, and waited for me. The tram was empty. It must have been about noon. It was hot; to right and left the houses slept in the sun. There were only a few dogs running round, and some chickens.

The conductress came towards me with her pouch, wanting money. That's right, I thought, the Romanians are our allies, we're supposed to pay. I shrugged and laughed. But she was quite serious. 'Nix,' she said firmly. Turning my wound towards her I said: 'Kaputt, see?' but that didn't move her. She shrugged her shoulders and rubbed thumb and forefinger. 'Nix,' she repeated. Digging into my haversack I found some writing paper, a few crushed

65

cigarettes that I intended to smoke in my pipe, the socks, and a pair of nail scissors. I showed her the nail scissors. The driver raced along at breakneck speed. Some other people had got on. The conductress attended to them, then came back. I showed her the scissors. 'How many *lei*?' I asked. She wrinkled her nose. She was quite pretty, and I could see that the scissors appealed to her. She snipped her nails with them, smiled at me, and indicated 'twenty' with her fingers. I nodded. I was so happy, for they couldn't touch me, maybe I was a hero, I'd been wounded right at the front, ten metres away from the Russians. The conductress gave me a ten-*lei* bill and the ticket for five *lei*. That was all. But I didn't mind. I was happy, they couldn't touch me.

I turned to look out at my surroundings. We passed a café, and I remembered I hadn't had anything to drink for two days and had a raging thirst. The tram stopped at a big square where there was a cinema for the military and some cafés and department stores. It was a busy scene, with soldiers milling round, and whores, and peddlers with their barrows. The whores were fantastically beautiful, with almond eyes and scarlet mouths, but they looked pretty pricey to me.

I got off and went into a café; no one paid any attention to me, no one saw the wound in my back, a superb wound, all bloody, with shreds of cloth and needing at least four months to heal. There was just one soldier in the café, sitting at the back, a corporal, and I could tell at once that he was drunk. To the left sat a man with black hair, coal black, and a fat, pale face, eating a pickled cucumber and smoking a black cigar. To the right sat a woman who smiled at me. She was smoking a cigarette, puffing fiendish smoke rings.

'Lover boy!' she called out, but I didn't like the looks of her, and I was sure she would be very pricey. The corporal at the back called out: 'Hey, there!' I walked towards him. His eyes were dim and unfocused. His chest was covered with medals, and he had a large carafe of wine in front of him.

'Help yourself!' he said. My God, how glorious it was to drink! I drank straight from the carafe. My God, how wonderful it was to drink! I could physically feel how parched I was, and it was a cool wine, on the dry side.

'Help yourself!' said the corporal, but the carafe was empty. 'Hey, pal!' he called out, and a greasy-looking fellow immediately came from behind a curtain, snatched up the carafe, and carried it off. The black-haired man was now sitting with the woman, who was as blonde as he was dark. He let her take a bite of his pickle and a puff of his cigar; then they both laughed, and the black-haired man called out towards the curtain something that sounded like Latin, a slushy kind of Latin.

The greasy youth arrived with the carafe, a bigger one than the last, and he also brought along another glass.

'Help yourself!' said the corporal.

He poured, and we drank. I drank, I drank, it was glorious, it was wonderful.

'Have a smoke,' said the corporal, but I hauled out my general's packet and slapped it onto the table. The blonde woman was laughing with the black-haired man; now they were drinking wine. Wine on top of pickles, I thought, that's asking for trouble, but they seemed to be enjoying it as they blew their fiendish smoke rings in the air.

'Drink away,' said the corporal. 'I have to go back to the front tonight, for the fifth time, goddammit!'

'Take the tram,' I said, 'I've just come from there, for the third time.'

'Where've you come from?'

'From the front.'

'Did you skedaddle?'

'No, I was wounded.'

'Oh, come on!'

I showed him my back.

'Goddammit,' he exclaimed, 'aren't you the lucky one! That's fantastic. Sell it to me!'

'Sell what?'

'That thing there, that red mess on your back – sell it to me!'

He slapped a whole pile of bills on the table, picked up the carafe, and lifted it to his mouth. Then I drank, then he, then I . . .

'Hey, pal!' he called.

The greasy youth reappeared and brought another carafe, and we drank.

'Sell it to me, you coward,' shouted the corporal. 'I'll give you a thousand *lei*, two thousand, three thousand, you can buy yourself the best-looking whores, and tobacco, and wine, and you . . .'

'But you can buy wounds right here, they made me an offer at the station.'

The corporal suddenly turned sober and grabbed my arm.

'Where?' he asked hoarsely.

'At the station,' I said, 'they made me an offer right there.'

'Hey, pal!' shouted the corporal. 'How much?' He slapped some money on the table, grabbed my arm, and said: 'Wait here.'

He put on his cap, tightened his belt and left.

The greasy youth brought another carafe. 'It's paid for,' he said with a grin. And I drank. The blonde woman was sitting on the black-haired man's knee, shrieking away. She had a cigar in her mouth and a cold pork chop in her hand. The black-haired man was already quite drunk. I drank and

68

smoked. It was glorious, I was drunk, wonderfully drunk, and I'd been wounded, and they couldn't touch me, maybe I was a hero. Wounded for the third time. The wine was glorious, glorious . . .

'Hey, pal!' I called out. The greasy youth came and stood grinning in front of me. I pulled the socks out of my haversack and held them out: 'How much wine?' He shrugged and wrinkled his nose, then took the socks and held them up to his face. 'Not new,' he said, sniffing with his long nose.

'How much?' I asked.

'Give you wine, two like that.' He pointed at the carafe.

'Bring it,' I said, 'bring it here, the wine.'

He brought it. Both carafes at once. I drank, I drank, it was glorious, it was wonderful, I was completely drunk, but as sober as only a happy man can be. It was indescribable how cool and dry the wine was, and I paid for it with two pairs of socks. The woman ate a second pork chop as she smoked a cigarette. She was a thin little creature and shrieked like crazy as she sat on the black-haired man's knee. I saw everything clear as clear, drunk though I was. I could see she wasn't wearing either a slip or underpants, and the black-haired man kept pinching her behind; that made her shriek, she shrieked because of that too. Then the black-haired man started yelling his head off, lifted the woman high in the air, and carried her out through the door.

At that moment the corporal walked in again.

'Help yourself!' I called out to him.

'Hey, pal!' shouted the corporal, whereupon the greasy youth appeared at once.

'Wine!' shouted the corporal. 'A whole barrel of wine!' and I knew that it had worked. He picked up my second carafe, drank it down at one go, and smashed it against the wall.

'Those fellows,' said the corporal, 'do a great job. Pistol with silencer. You stand round a corner and stick out your paw, and plop – take a look.'

He pulled up his sleeve. They had put a nice clean hole through his forearm, bandaged it, and even supplied him with a casualty certificate.

The greasy youth brought a large carafe. The corporal was beside himself, shouting and drinking, shouting and drinking. And said: 'My name's Hubert.'

And I drank; it was wonderful.

Then we went off to the first-aid station. Hubert knew all the ropes. As we arrived, a few freight cars were just being loaded with minor casualties. There were two doctors, and in front of each stood a long queue of walking wounded. Since we were drunk, we wanted to come last. We joined the second queue because that doctor looked kinder than the other one. A corporal stood beside him calling out 'Next!' Some cases took a long time, and those who had been treated walked through a long corridor leading to a courtyard.

We sat down on a bench, since we were drunk and rather unsteady on our legs. Next to me sat a man who'd had a bullet through the palm of his hand, clear through it, and he was bleeding like a pig onto the bench. He was quite grey in the face.

The doctors were working with the door open, cigarettes between their lips, and sometimes they would take a pull from a bottle. They were slaving away like crazy, and the one I was queuing up for had a nice face, an intelligent face, and I noticed he had skilful, quiet hands. A vehicle arrived with some serious casualties, and we had to wait. The corporal shut the door, and we could hear screams, and there was an even stronger smell of blood and ether. The man with the injured hand had fallen asleep and had stopped bleeding. The blood from his hand had gone all over me, and when I took my paybook out of my left pocket I found it soaked in blood; the first few pages were no longer legible. I was drunk, I didn't care, and they couldn't, they couldn't touch me, they couldn't get at me, I'd been wounded, I'd been wounded right at the front, and maybe I was even a hero.

So now I was the unknown soldier.

I said aloud to myself, 'I am the unknown soldier,' but the others, sitting on the ground or on the bench, called out 'Shut up!' I shut up and looked out onto the street. Hubert had fallen asleep, with his arm stuck out stiffly; it looked very impressive, like a genuine battle injury. They had done a good job; I must be sure and ask him how much it cost. And if the war wasn't over in four months, I'd get them to shoot me through the arm, too, then I'd get the gold badge, then I'd be a proper official hero, and they wouldn't be able to touch me at all. But now he was asleep, they still hadn't finished with the six stretcher cases, and all we could hear was their screaming. I wasn't all that drunk any more. Someone in the queue suddenly asked quietly: 'Got a smoke, anyone?' I recognized the man with the leg who had supported himself on his rifle. But he didn't recognize me. He still had his rifle, and his face was the face of a real hero. He was proud. I gave him a few of the general's cigarettes. Hubert was sound asleep and snoring; now his face was quite happy. Then the door opened, and the corporal called out again, 'Next!'

After that everything went very fast, and no more vehicles arrived. I was still drunk after all, but I felt fine, with no pain to speak of.

'Hey, next, it's your turn!' the corporal shouted.

I stepped into a classroom where the benches had been piled up and Marshal Antonescu looked down from the wall, together with Crown Prince Michael. There was a disgusting smell of blood and ether. I took off my tunic and shirt, unaided; I was still drunk. 'Hurry up!' said the corporal. Crown Prince Michael had a really stupid Hohenzollern face, and he was boss over the black-haired people and the whores and the greasy youths, the onions and the pickles and the wine. But Romania was a real mess, and he'd never bring it off, nor would Antonescu.

At that moment I became perfectly sober, for the doctor was snipping away in my back. I could feel nothing as he had given me a local anaesthetic, but it is a very queer sensation when they snip away in you like that. I could see it all quite clearly: in front of me was a big glass-doored cupboard and behind me a glass instrument-case. And I could see my smooth back and the big hole in it, and the doctor snipping the edges nice and smooth and picking something out of the hole. I felt like a frozen carcass being divided up between two butchers. His snipping was quick and deft; then he dabbed something onto the wound, and I saw that the hole had become much bigger. Go on, make it a little bigger, I thought, then it'll take six months. Maybe the doctor was thinking the same thing. Once again he started snipping and probing. Then came more dabbing, and the corporal, who had been holding me as a matter of routine, went to the door and called out, 'Next!'

'Hand grenade, was it, my boy?' the doctor asked as he placed a large wad of cotton wool on the hole in my back.

'I think so,' I replied.

'Quite a nice long piece, want to keep it?' He held out a crumpled, bloodied strip of metal.

'No, thanks,' I said. He tossed it in the garbage can, and I could see a leg lying there, a real, perfectly good, splendid leg. I was cold sober.

'I'm sure there's a bit of wood in there still, and some shreds of cloth, they'll all have to come out with the pus – just make certain nothing stays behind.' He laughed. The corporal bandaged me up, winding all kinds of stuff round me, and now dammit I really did feel like a hero, goddammit, wounded by a hand grenade, right at the front.

The doctor looked at Hubert's clean hole, then at the corporal, and his expression became serious. 'Made to order, my friend, just made to order.'

I felt hot all over, but Hubert remained cool.

'A really magnificent home-leave shot, that's the fifth today,' said the corporal.

'Magnificent,' said the doctor, but he didn't touch it, merely glanced at the corporal, and the corporal, who was still bandaging me, went across to have a good look at it; then he too looked at Hubert. 'Magnificent,' he said.

The doctor, sitting with his legs crossed, was smoking a cigarette. He didn't touch the wound. Hubert was quite calm but no longer drunk.

'What's going on?' he asked in surprise. 'May I go now – out that way? Be seeing you, Hans,' he said to me. He actually started to leave.

'Hold it,' said the doctor. 'What d'you think you're doing! Baumüller?' He turned towards the corporal who had bandaged me. I was all through now and put on my belt with the haversack.

'It stinks,' said the corporal. 'Made to order.'

'Coming, Hubert?' I asked.

'You two know each other?' asked the doctor.

'My section leader,' I said calmly, 'he was lying right beside me . . .'

'I see,' said the doctor; the corporal who had bandaged me also said, 'I see,' and they believed me because I had such a splendid hole in my back, a hero's hole. We left.

Hubert pressed my hand.

Standing outside on the railway tracks were three freight cars. In another car men were singing, and there was that authentic smell of railway, of coal and dry wood, as in all railway stations in the world. There was a smell of war. And it was too bad that we were no longer even slightly drunk. Hubert jumped into a car and helped me up, for I was a bit stiff what with all that bandaging; besides, I now had a huge hole in my back. From his left and right pockets he pulled out a bottle, thrust one at me, and shouted triumphantly: 'There – drink, drink!' and we drank . . . and it was wonderful, they couldn't touch us, we were wounded, properly wounded, maybe we were heroes, and the corporal would get the gold badge, and then they wouldn't be able to touch him at all.

The train started. It would travel through the Carpathians, through the *puszta*, through all of Hungary, all the way to the Vienna Woods.

But first only a few kilometres to the main station, where we received rations: white bread, cheese, and tobacco. Coffee too, but we had no mess-tins. Then blankets were distributed, and we bedded down very comfortably in the freight car. There were only twenty-four of us: it was a French car, and below the inscription: '8 chevaux, 40 hommes' some joker had written: '1/2 elephant, 20,000 white mice.' I had to laugh. We were all classified as 'minor casualties'. I had hoped to be among the so-called 'stretcher cases', since those were conveyed home later in white beds

74

in a hospital train. But the doctor at the railway station had said I was a 'minor casualty'. We were twelve at each end, six a side, and in the middle was an empty space with pots of coffee and mugs. We drank coffee and ate white bread and cheese. Dusk began falling, and the train moved off.

The doctor who had divided us at the station into 'minor casualties' and 'stretcher cases' had put Hubert in charge of our car. Hubert assigned us our places and distributed the blankets, and before the train left he hauled a keg of wine on board. 'Help yourselves!' he cried.

The dusk deepened as we travelled across a grey plain with grazing land and huge herds of cattle. Herdsmen's fires stood out against the flat horizon, and the fires and black smoke from gypsy camps hung in the sky like great banners; the gypsies were singing, we supposed, and we drank. Each man had received a litre of wine, and we were all getting drunk. We were once more in a casualty train, and I was a hero, I would get the silver badge and Hubert the gold; it was his fifth time. One by one the others fell asleep, and I sat alone with Hubert on a wooden crate by the open door, and we drank up the wine, smoked, and didn't say a word.

The sky was grey and beneath it stretched shimmering, cool-green maize fields, and often we were travelling across the steppe and could hear the lowing of the herds, see the quiet fires of the herdsmen. Sometimes we would pass through a station where people were standing waiting for trains going the other way, soldiers and Romanians in colourful costumes, and I thought how terrible it must be for the soldiers to be standing there and going off to the front. It would have been nice if we could have told them where to find the sellers of home-leave shots; then they could immediately have taken the train home again from that station. But no doubt most of them would have been scared. I would have been scared. I know I would have been scared to do something like that, and to me Hubert was a hero. Goddammit, that required courage.

'You're a hero,' I said in a low voice.

'Shut up.'

Then darkness fell, but the sky was still grey, a soft grey, with the tall poles of the draw-wells outlined against it like black screams of torment. Villages lay silent and patient in their maize fields under the grey sky, and I had no desire to sleep: it was so glorious, it was wonderful, and the most wonderful thing was that they couldn't touch me. We smoked and drank, and neither said a word.

The train stopped at a lighted station, and we could see it was a big one. We halted beside a regular platform that was crowded with people, some of them in rags, but there were also some very smart Romanian officers with their whores, and Romanian soldiers who got paid in beatings. In a freight car somewhere up front, the stretcher cases were screaming horribly.

The crowd on the platform parted, and two doctors and a corporal approached. Beside me Hubert whistled through his teeth. 'We're being screened,' he said. Grabbing the empty keg he disappeared behind me, getting down off the train on the side where the tracks were. And I looked right into the solemn faces of the people on the platform and felt myself to be a hero. Up front they were still screaming; I saw from my watch that it was only eleven thirty, and here I'd been thinking the night was almost over.

The doctors entered our car. 'On your feet!' one of them shouted, 'everybody on their feet!' I felt calm enough but was aware of the tension in the others. I presented myself first. 'Right,' he said. 'Any pain?' 'Yes,' I said. 'A pill,

Schwitzkowski.' The corporal gave me a pill. The next man was kicked out; he only had a tiny splinter in his arm and hadn't even bled. The doctor shone his flashlight onto each wound. It was dark and silent in the car. Several times he said: 'Out!', and those to whom he said 'Out!' got out right away and had to wait on the platform. Finally he went over to the corner where a man was lying quite still.

'Get up, damn you!' said the doctor. But the man just lay there and said nothing. Perhaps he's dead, I thought. 'What's the matter with you?' shouted the doctor. Now the man said quietly: 'Shot in the leg.'

'But you're a stretcher case – what are you doing here? Let's have a look.' He kneeled down and turned the wounded man onto his stomach. 'There?' he asked. 'Here?' he asked, and each time the wounded man groaned. 'Come on now,' said the doctor, 'don't be a sissy.' Then he said: 'Carry him out, put him in with the stretcher cases.' Two men picked him up, and the corporal shone his flashlight.

As they carried him past me, I saw that he was already dead. It was quite obvious – he was dead. 'But he's dead,' I told the corporal. 'Shut up,' he replied, and they carried him out, and the people on the platform made room. One of the Romanian officers touched his cap. He must have also seen that the man was dead. Back there in the corner, the doctor had poked and prodded him to death.

Someone came and asked how many of us were left. We had to count off, and in the dark I counted off in two different voices. There were still fourteen of us. They brought us some hot milk and a few Romanian cigarettes each. Then we started off again. At the last moment Hubert jumped back on from the far side. There was another man with him who laughed and said there was nothing wrong with him, just that he was almost blind and had broken his

77

glasses. He had a certificate from his lieutenant saying that his glasses had been broken by 'enemy action'. The half-blind man lay down somewhere in the corner, and Hubert gave him the milk I had been saving for him. We two drank the schnapps he had brought along.

After the hot milk they all needed to go, and for a long time we had no peace on our wooden crate. It was getting chilly, too, and by that time it was quite dark.

In the silent fields we were passing, something seemed to be lying in wait. And the humped villages sleeping among the bushes seemed dangerous.

The apricot brandy was very strong, and when it hit the hot milk I suddenly felt miserably sick. At every rattle, the vomit rose to my throat and slipped down again, and the dark-grey fields became a blur, a whirling mush, before my eyes. I threw up. I grabbed a blanket and lay down on the straw, and Hubert pushed another blanket under my head for a pillow. He said nothing. It was uncannily quiet.

I fell asleep. When I woke up I was shivering.

It was not yet light, and the train had halted in a narrow gorge. Hubert was standing outside smoking a cigarette. 'Hallo there!' he called. 'Had a good sleep?' I lit a cigarette and got down off the train too. Most of the minor casualties were standing outside. On either side were very steep mountains, and high up, very high up, I saw a young herdsman, a boy, waving his hat. I took off my cap and waved back at him.

The boy shouted something, probably he was very lonely up there and glad when a train passed. I suddenly felt hungry, climbed back into the freight car, and ate up the rest of the white bread and the cheese and drank some cold coffee with it. I wasn't a bit happy any more, I longed to be home. My wound was hurting how, and I could tell that it had begun to fester; I felt very sick. I looked forward to a bed, and I wouldn't have minded a wash. I hadn't washed for three days. We had been marching, attacking, marching, attacking, the food lorry had had a direct hit; then I'd been wounded and since then I'd been boozing: no wonder I was feeling sick. One man stood right beside me and pissed against the inside wall of the car.

'Hey!' I cried. 'What d'you think you're doing?'

'I'm pissing,' he replied calmly.

'Piss properly, then!'

'I am pissing properly.' I was about to get up and show him how to piss, but it was too late – he'd finished and was already buttoning his trousers. Then I saw that it was the half-blind man and thought, he's putting it on.

I picked up my blanket and lay down somewhere else, feeling wretched, and now I wasn't thinking that they couldn't get at me but wondering instead how I could get at them.

The engine whistled, and we crawled over one of those uncomfortably swaying Carpathian bridges; then we came to a station where we were screened all over again. Hubert disappeared as he'd done before. But this time they got the half-blind man, and a few others too. One of them merely had eczema.

'Eczema!' said the doctor. 'Are you crazy, to go all the way back to Hungary with eczema?'

By this time there were only eight of us left, and they moved us from three freight cars into one. It was odd that once again we were exactly twenty-four. Maybe all they had was that one car. The man with eczema and the half-blind fellow and all the simple bullet holes had to stay behind just because there was only one car. From among the stretcher cases they carried out those who were no longer fit to be

79

transported. Of one of them there was very little left anyway. He was minus both legs, and it looked like very little when they carried the stretcher past us. He was as white as milk in the face but looked furious, and his bandages were black with blood. They also carried away a body, the man the doctor in our car had poked and prodded to death.

I still felt ghastly, and once again the freight car was crowded. A very stern corporal had been put in charge. He was tall and broad and wore the Cross of Merit, and I was sure he was a schoolteacher and just about to be promoted to sergeant.

'To your places!' he shouted. He suffered from jaundice, and his fat face looked like a bronze statue of Mussolini.

'Sit down!' he shouted.

'Count off!' We counted off.

I simply missed out one number and said 'fourteen' instead of 'thirteen', and he didn't notice because he forgot to count himself. No one noticed. We were all tired and hungry, and our wounds had begun to hurt.

Then we were given white bread and cheese and some hot coffee. I was worried about Hubert, couldn't see him anywhere, but the engine was there and it looked as if we were going to leave any minute.

I got out, and the stern corporal asked where I was going, saying no one was allowed to get out. I said I had to have a shit; he couldn't do anything about that so he told me to be quick about it.

Walking over to the station building I called out: 'Hubert!' I found him in the little bar next to the waiting-room. He was drunk. 'I'm changing my money,' he called out. 'We're going to Hungary, you have to have *pengö* there. Come along, sit down!'

80

We had a clear view of the train, and I saw the stern corporal sticking his head out of the car several times.

'They've counted off.'

'So what?'

'But he's strict, that *Kapo*.'

'So what?'

'And the fellow in charge, a doctor, knows exactly how many of us there are.'

'So what?'

He was very drunk.

'But what are you going to do? You're one too many!'

'I've already spoken to the doctor.'

A girl brought a big hunk of roast pork and some bread; it smelled fantastic and must have cost a lot. We ate, drank some wine, and I thought, well, if he's spoken to the doctor, nothing can happen to him, and I felt fine again. We bought some tobacco and a few more bottles of wine, then walked back to our freight car. Right after that the train left.

The stern corporal asked Hubert: 'What are you doing here? You don't belong in here.'

'I beg to differ, I've always been in here.'

'That's not true.'

'Hey, fellows!' Hubert called out. 'Haven't I always been in here?'

Most of the men were silent and said nothing, but the eight who had been in our old car called out: 'Of course he belongs in here!'

'But we've only reported twenty-four,' said the stern corporal.

'That was a mistake.'

'We don't make mistakes.'

'But it was a mistake.'

'We really were twenty-five before,' I said.

81

'Shut up!'

'Because you didn't count yourself,' I said.

'You're drunk!' shouted the stern corporal, and now I knew that he really was a schoolteacher.

'This business has to be cleared up,' he told Hubert.

'It's been cleared up,' Hubert said as he sat down.

'I am responsible.'

'You're an arsehole.'

'How dare you speak to me like that in front of the troops!'

'Because you are one.'

'I'll report it to the doctor.'

'I've already reported it to the doctor.'

'Reported what?'

'That you're an arsehole.'

Everyone laughed, and the stern corporal sat down too. By now it was somewhere round eight or nine in the morning. I felt great, and we drank wine. What I could see of the outside seemed to me already quite Hungarian, but we were still in Romania. There were peasants in the fields, and they waved their hats and called out something that sounded Hungarian.

But then we stopped at a station in a big city, and true enough we were still in Romania. I was appalled at the thought that we might be dropped off here so that I wouldn't even get as far back as Hungary.

Now the doctor will come, I thought, and Hubert hasn't spoken to the doctor of course, and it's all going to come out.

The doctor arrived, quite young. He was laughing – probably glad to have been assigned to this train and so able to travel with us, maybe even as far as the Vienna Woods.

'How's it going, boys?' he called. 'Anyone here in pain?' And just as the stern corporal was about to open his mouth, Hubert and the doctor looked at each other and they both laughed. 'Kramer!' the doctor exclaimed. 'What the hell are you doing here? Did you stop one again?'

'Yes, Berghannes, I did.' He jumped off the train and walked up and down the platform with the doctor. The stern corporal looked pretty foolish, but then food was delivered which he had to dole out. White bread and cheese and another roll of fruit-drops, and I ate hungrily. Hubert and the doctor paced up and down the platform until the train was about to move off.

'Shit,' he said. 'We'll just barely enter Hungary.'

'Who says so?'

'The doctor.'

'Shit.'

'Right, maybe there's something we can do about it,' he said with a laugh.

'Like what, for instance?'

'We might be able to join the stretcher cases when some of them have to be unloaded again.'

'Then we'll go as far as the Vienna Woods.'

'Like hell Vienna Woods – the whole train's only going as far as Debrecen.'

'Okay, so Debrecen's quite near Budapest.'

'Let's hope we can work it.'

'Is the doctor a good friend of yours?'

'We were at university together.'

Christ, I thought, he's been to university. I said no more. He held out a bottle to me. The train was now moving into the Carpathians, right into the very heart of them. It was warm, and the schnapps tasted deliciously of apricots.

'Why so silent?'

'Oh . . .'

'Come on, what's up?'

83

'I was just thinking that you're kind of a highbrow if you've been to university.'

'Hell no – don't imagine there's anything so special about universities! What d'you do for a living?'

'I'm a stove-fitter.'

'You should be proud you can fit a stove properly so that it draws and people keep warm and can cook on it. I tell you, that's a fine craft, an admirable one, my friend. Here, drink, take a good swig.' I took a good swig.

'But at the big universities they learn how to be doctors and judges and teachers, that's a pretty high-class bunch of people,' I said.

'Much too high-class. The point is, they're only high-class because they go round with their noses in the air, that's all. To hell with them.'

'Are you a doctor or a teacher or a judge?'

'Not me – I never finished, I wanted to be a teacher, but they made me a soldier.'

'Well, sure, they can't use the stupidest ones at university . . .'

'Don't you believe it – sometimes they like those the best.'

'I don't believe it.'

He pointed to the stern corporal, saying: 'Just look at that fellow: there you have a solid citizen. He believes that everything he does is for the good of the state, but actually all he's concerned with is his citizen's stomach and his arse. He likes to eat well and is a bit of a coward. And likes to bawl people out. The fact is, he's concerned only with himself. He's scared that, because I got into the train, he might be kicked out since he only has jaundice while I've been honourably wounded. Haven't I?'

'Of course.'

'There you are, then. The state likes these fellows,

although it knows they're concerned only with themselves. It gives them a job where they have something to say but also something to lose, and that takes care of it. To hell with all that. They'll be surprised to see what I'm capable of.'

He drank again from the bottle, and I wondered whether he might have been overdoing the booze a bit.

'What d'you think you're doing there?' he called out to the stern corporal, who was working something out on a piece of paper on his knee.

'Counting my assault days and my close-combat days,' he said, modestly enough.

'What assault days?'

'*My* assault days.'

'Where the hell did you take part in an assault or close combat?'

'Up there near Kishinev – you know.'

'Kishinev? Which unit?'

'The tank corps . . .'

'And that's where you were in close combat and an assault? You look like a pretty fierce fighter to me, I must say!'

The stern corporal blushed. And I was tempted to feel sorry for him.

'Well,' he said, 'if you like I can show you. On three assault days I was up at the front, taking round food, bringing back wounded . . .'

'You're a bastard, I tell you – you ate up the men's rations and pinched the valuables out of the wounded men's pockets. That's the kind of chap you are.'

'How dare you speak to me like that! Cut it out, you're drunk.'

'Sure I am, drunks tell the truth. That's the kind of bastard you are. Here,' he said suddenly, ripping all the decorations off his chest, 'take the Iron Cross and the assault badge and the close-combat badge, I've had it up to here with them.'

By now he was totally drunk. I grabbed hold of him and laid him down flat on his blanket.

'You can see he's plastered, can't you?' I said.

The stern corporal said nothing. I picked up the decorations from the floor and put them in my pocket. No one said a word.

We were now travelling through some marvellous scenery, magnificent mountains and picturesque villages and small towns. It was almost noon, and we began to eat our white bread and our tinned cheese, and we were all thirsty. We stopped at a small station, and someone asked the corporal whether we might try and get something to drink.

'I'm not saying another word.' He seemed to be still working something out on his knee. 'I'm not saying anything any more. I ate up all your rations and pinched your valuables from your pockets. I'm not saying another word.'

I almost think he was close to tears, and now I was quite sure he was a schoolteacher.

'Don't be an idiot,' someone called out, 'he was drunk!'

'Drunks tell the truth . . .'

'*Kapo*, don't be such a fool,' came another voice, 'he was just being mean!'

'No, I'm a bastard.'

'Come on, there's a good lad, we don't believe him!'

'I didn't do my duty.'

'You did, you did – come on, chin up. Look, he's plastered.'

'So can we go and get something to drink?'

'It's against regulations, and if the train suddenly starts to move you'll miss it – but then I'm not responsible. He knows all the doctors intimately, and he sized me up right away.'

A few men got off the train, hurried to a nearby house, and came back with some water and some weak coffee. They first let the corporal have a drink. One man wanted to fill up a whole mug for him.

'Hold it,' said the corporal, 'don't forget your mates.'

Then the others got off too, and he said with a laugh: 'I'm not responsible any more – it feels good not to be responsible any more! The man responsible is asleep and drunk. He has the right attitude towards duty.'

They all looked angrily at the sleeping Hubert. He slept very quietly, but his face showed some stress, and now for the first time I had a good look at him. He was older than I, at least six or seven years older. At least twenty-five. He had very fair hair and a narrow face and didn't look well, but then he'd been drinking pretty heavily the last few days.

Then the young doctor returned and called out: 'Kramer!' I pointed at Hubert, and the doctor said: 'Let him sleep.' Then he told us: 'It's all right for you fellows to get off here for a bit, the engine's broken down. It may take a while.'

It was a very small station. The station building looked half asleep; it smelled of resin and ripe maize. There were piles of lumber lying around, and stacks of iron and indefinable objects such as seemed to have been left at almost every station. The train stood there without an engine like a snake without a head. Not a soul in sight.

I sniffed the air and suddenly smelled that it was Sunday. There was a smell of inactivity. I walked past the station, where they were all converging like flies onto the bar.

There was such a glorious smell of summer and Sunday, and then I heard sobbing violin music that drove me wild. There wasn't a dog to be seen in the dusty street, not a soul in sight.

Aha, I thought, they've filled their bellies with goulash

and now they're sleeping it off, and someone's playing the violin. The music was coming from a tiny bar, and suddenly I realized I was thirsty and went inside.

All I saw there were a few swarthy fellows sitting on dilapidated chairs; they didn't really look in too good shape, they were very thin and sallow, and I thought maybe they hadn't been eating goulash after all. Another man was leaning against the bar producing sobbing sounds from his violin.

I stared in amazement at the violin, surely tears must be pouring down it, but it was quite dry. And the men all looked terribly parched too. Maybe because of all that paprika, I thought. I had never been to Hungary, and I imagined they all ate a lot of paprika and goulash and made their violins sob. Only the mouth of the plump, pretty woman behind the bar was moist, and as I entered and called out 'Hallo, comrades!' they laughed and responded with some friendly-sounding Hungarian words; the woman was especially welcoming with her friendly '*Gooter Tak!*'

I walked towards the bar. The fellow went on playing his violin and gave me a pleasant smile.

'Might I please have a glass of water?' I asked very politely, not having a penny in my pocket. The woman laughed, the way we sometimes laugh when someone speaks an incomprehensible language. Then she said, with a cooing sound like a pigeon's in her lovely, smooth throat: '*Bor.*'

But I didn't know what she meant, and I told her so. That made her laugh even more, and delightful dimples appeared in her handsome face. Then she said: '*Birr.*'

I shook my head and said: 'No *pengö*,' and stubbornly went on asking for water. Meanwhile I had put my hands in my pockets and was listening to the young violinist. The others, too, were listening to him spellbound, smiling only when I

88

caught their eyes. In my pocket, however, I found a brand-new, factory-fresh Wehrmacht handkerchief, one of those olive-green ones, and holding it out to the woman I asked: 'How many *pengö* this?'

But she shook her head at once, and I realized I was no longer in Romania. In Romania you could sell anyone anything. A shadow crossed the woman's face, and I felt sad too because I thought I had offended her, but she was soon smiling again, set a bottle and glass on a table, and gestured to me to sit down. 'You no *pengö*,' she said encouragingly.

I sat down beside one of the swarthy fellows and listened to the sobbing violin.

I found it cruelly sad and beautiful; it seemed to smell of passionate kisses and tears shed over a broken heart. I could feel my tears welling up, but then I opened the bottle and poured some wonderful brown beer into the glass. My mouth watered. At that moment the violinist paused briefly, and I rose, held up my glass, and called out: 'First, my Hungarian comrades, let me drink to the loveliest of all women,' raising my glass to the landlady.

'And then,' I went on with a nod towards the violinist: 'let me drink to you, comrade, you who can sob like a god. I'm not making fun of you, far from it, but keep up the sobbing and to hell with everything else. And now let me drink to the whole parched Hungarian people – don't be offended, but I don't know what else to say.'

And I drank down the whole huge, glorious glassful, and it tasted so good that I almost choked with pleasure.

My speech met with loud approval. They seemed to have understood me, and they laughed like children as they raised their glasses to me.

One of them came up and filled my glass; I had to drink it

89

down in one go. They immediately produced another bottle, and I finished that off in short order, too. The beer was truly glorious, and it was so warm outside, and it was summer, and I was in Hungary, and they couldn't touch me, and I would have no trouble hearing the train whistle and could quickly run out and jump on. I was soon slightly drunk and sorry I didn't have any money for treating my Hungarian friends in return. But they merely smiled when I tried through gestures to indicate my problem, and the landlady was especially nice to me. I think she liked me, I liked her, too, although she was much older than I, but she was kind and generous and she was a handsome woman, a fine figure of a Hungarian innkeeper . . .

After the fourth bottle I began heaping abuse on Hitler. 'Comrades,' I called out dramatically, 'Hitler is an arsehole!' They fully agreed and stamped their feet in delight. The sobbing violinist was quite carried away by my speech; he picked up his violin and produced some frantic revolutionary sobbing, his fingers scampering up and down the strings at breakneck speed.

Suddenly one of my new pals grabbed my arm: 'Ssh, ssh!' he went, and everyone fell silent. From the direction of the station I could hear loud shouting. I felt a bit sick to my stomach, but then I thought, only bad people are ever in a hurry. I stood up: 'Comrades, the hour of farewell has struck. Don't be offended, but the fact is I'd like to get as far as possible to the rear, to a hospital and close to Germany, otherwise I'll be sitting here all summer, drinking beer and listening to the violin. Don't be offended.'

They fully understood and urged me to get going. I hurried over to the landlady and tried to kiss her hand, but she gave me a playful shove. . .

The avenue was lovely and cool, yet there was a smell of

summer and Sunday and of Hungary. Dense chestnut trees that looked as rich and thick as that glorious beer. I soon noticed how drunk I was; the avenue seemed to sway ever so slightly.

The train was still there. At first I couldn't see anyone about, but then someone called out, 'There he is!' and I saw all the men from the two freight cars lined up, the doctor facing them. The doctor, Hubert's old pal, was angry, angry and upset, and I imagined it was because of me, because I'd been away, but that wasn't it at all. 'Where've you been?' he asked sternly, but without waiting for a reply he said: 'Fall in!'

I obeyed, and the others laughed because it was obvious that I was good and drunk. The doctor looked at us solemnly, then glanced at a sheet of paper and said somewhat dramatically:

'Men, I have some information that will interest you all. We received it over the radio as a special announcement, and I have no wish to withhold it from you.'

He gave us all another solemn look and continued:

'Today, in the early hours of the morning, the joint British–American forces landed on the west coast of France. A battle of the utmost violence is in progress. In this solemn hour, comrades, when the cowardly liars are finally confronting us, we will not fail to utter a threefold "Sieg Heil!" to our Führer, to whom we owe everything. Comrades – Sieg . . .' – '. . . Heil!' we shouted. He repeated it twice with us. Then you could hear a pin drop, and into that silence Hubert suddenly shouted: 'Hurrah, hurrah, hurrah!' We looked up, startled and horrified, including the doctor. Hubert was standing half-asleep by the doorway of the car, deep lines in his face and wisps of straw clinging to his tunic.

'What's that supposed to mean, Kramer?' the doctor shouted furiously.

'Sir, because at least they're confronting us, you see – that's why I'm shouting hurrah. Now we'll defeat them, wipe them out, and then the war will be over – hurrah, hurrah, hurrah!'

He was grinning from ear to ear, and the doctor and the rest of us laughed too.

'Dismiss!' said the doctor, 'everyone stay with the train – the engine will be here any minute.'

Hubert jumped down from the car and walked over to the doctor; I could see them chatting together. The others crept back into the car; some of them sat down on the stacks of iron, ate their bread and cheese, and drank cold coffee, since they had no *pengö*.

I stayed close to the station exit, waiting for Hubert; my idea was for him to give me some money or come with me so we could treat those parched fellows and the violinist until the landlady was down to the last bottle of that glorious beer.

Hubert slapped me on the shoulder and told me quietly: 'Two more hours at least, but I'm not supposed to tell anyone. Are you drunk?'

'Yes.'

'What from?'

'Beer.'

'Any good?'

'Fantastic,' I replied.

'Let's go,' said Hubert, 'where's this place of yours?'

We slipped away quickly, but as soon as we reached the lovely cool avenue we slowed down. It was warm and summery, and we'd been wounded, and they couldn't touch us, we were in a proper hospital train – oh God, how wonderful it all was.

'Listen,' said Hubert as we walked on. 'D'you know that we have a genuine, bona fide reason to get drunk?'

'No,' I answered.

'Hell,' he said, 'they've landed, that means the end is near, I tell you – inexorably near. Now at least the end's no longer out of sight.'

'The end of the war?' I asked.

'Of course. Now the end is near, just wait and see.'

Suddenly Hubert stopped and grabbed my arm. 'Quiet!' We could hear the sobbing violin.

'That's in the bar,' I said with a laugh.

'In *our* bar?'

'Right!' I said, and Hubert again: 'Hurrah, hurrah, hurrah!' Now we were running.

The parched men welcomed us with loud laughter, even the violinist broke off his playing and nodded at me. And the landlady, my plump, handsome landlady, was positively delighted to see me again. I could tell. I made a short speech introducing my friend Hubert, and they all took him to their hearts. Hubert ordered seven bottles of beer for the three parched ones, for the violinist, for the landlady and for the two of us. He slapped a whole bundle of notes onto the table, and I could see from the eyes of the parched ones, those big, shyly glancing eyes, that the men were poor, and I was touched that they had paid for my beer.

Hubert went round filling all the glasses, then jumped onto a chair and raised his own.

'Men,' he cried, 'and this delightful lady, beg pardon! Is it not a thing of glory that we're all human beings? Is it not wonderful that we are brothers, and is it not disgusting that those pigs started the war in which they want to kill us off? But we're human beings, and we're going to take our revenge by continuing to be brothers, by stealing from them and screwing them – begging your pardon, fair lady – screwing them blind! Mates!' he cried, 'Hungarian mates, we're human beings, never forget that. And now let's drink!'

He emptied his glass, and an expression of amazement spread over his face. 'I'll be damned!' he exclaimed. 'This beer is truly magnificent!'

Everyone got carried away in their enthusiasm. We embraced each other, and I had a notion I might be able to kiss our lovely landlady, but she pushed me away with a laugh, and I saw that she was blushing.

Damn it, I thought, what a bastard you are – she's married and loves her husband, and you young whippersnapper want to kiss her. And then I stood up and gave another little speech in which I apologized and called myself a bastard. They all understood, including the landlady, who gave me a forgiving smile.

The Hungarians made speeches too, saying that we were brothers and Hitler and Horthy were bastards, and they spat on the floor and sprinkled some beer over it. Each time the landlady brought more beer she chalked seven strokes on a blackboard, and I soon saw that there were quite a lot of strokes. We had a great time, all of us, and told each other the most fantastic stories without understanding a word, and we understood each other famously.

The violinist sobbed out a piece that sounded like wine and silk, dark silk and heavy wine, and when he had finished Hubert suddenly shouted: 'Tokay!' But now we noticed that the woman was no longer there. Hubert gently took the violinist's instrument from him and led him to a chair, where he fell asleep at once.

I had a clear view of Hubert slipping a wad of notes into the violinist's pocket. Hubert really did have a fantastic amount of money, and I decided to ask him later on what he had flogged. Hubert picked up the violin and started to play; the parched ones danced in time to his music.

Actually I felt like making another speech, there was so much I wanted to say, but I simply didn't know how to begin.

The landlady returned with a platter of sliced cold meat and bread, and we ate as she watched us with a happy smile. The parched ones tucked in quite nicely, and I realized that they were hungry, really hungry, and it all tasted wonderful, the cold meat and the white bread, and we drank wine as we ate, and meanwhile I learned that *bor* meant wine, the only Hungarian word I knew.

We left some bread and meat on a plate for the violinist, and I spread my new green handkerchief over it to keep away the flies. After our meal, two of the parched ones fell asleep, sinking back into their chairs and closing their eyes; they were gone, sound asleep, and I thought of how hard they must have worked all week, somewhere in the forest, cutting wood or on the farms.

Finally Hubert got up and said: 'We have to go now.' He went over to the bar, and the woman counted up all the strokes and did a lengthy calculation.

I made another quick trip outside to the back and thought it was nice of the handsome landlady to follow me. She looked at me sadly and said some tender words as she stroked my hand; I was sure it was some kind of nonsense, the kind of thing women say to very small children. And then all of a sudden she kissed me on the lips, and I saw her blush deeply before she quickly disappeared again into the bar.

I went out through the garden, and I found the avenue more beautiful than ever. Once again I was drunk and the Hungarian woman had given me a fleeting kiss! I think I must have been in love with her, but I no longer know whether I was in love with her or with that lovely fleeting kiss – not that it matters, I was very happy, and I suddenly felt terribly young because I was drunk and wounded, and now I could feel my whole back sticky with pus.

The avenue was beautiful, and I wished it would never end. There was a sweet and slightly dusty smell of Hungary, of summer and Sunday, and I was as pleased as Punch that my wound was festering, I just didn't want it to heal quickly! I would go on drinking, for then it wouldn't heal so fast because the blood goes bad – yes, they'd told me all that in hospital the first time I was wounded, but in Germany there was no booze to be had, and that time my wound had healed up quickly.

The train looked horrible, standing there all sober on the rails, in the heat of the afternoon, and I felt depressed and wanted to go back and kiss the Hungarian woman all over again.

I was pretty drunk, I realized, when suddenly the engine whistled and I had to run. In jumping up I stumbled and made a grab for something, and that made my dressing split open. I could feel the warm pus running down my back into my pants.

They all laughed when I ran my hand down my back and over the seat of my trousers as if I had shit in my pants. I got out of my tunic and pulled off my shirt.

I lay face down on a straw pallet. With a flourish, Hubert threw my shirt out of the train. '*That*'ll fertilize the Hungarian earth!' he cried.

The other corporal kneeled down beside me and cleaned up the rest of the goo, then put on a dressing. I had never been so skilfully bandaged. After packing a thick, clean tampon into the hole in my back, he wrapped it all up neatly with gauze and finally wound a whole roll of bandage round me, fastening it on my chest. 'That's what we call a rucksack dressing,' he told me.

Hubert looked at him. 'Here,' he said, 'shake, you old arsehole.' They shook hands and laughed.

'I'll stand you all some schnapps,' my corporal called out, 'and we'll have a song.'

He passed round the bottle, and a fat infantryman asked: 'What are we going to sing?'

'Come, ye harlots of Damascus!' Hubert suggested.

So we sang that fine song: *'Come, ye harlots of Damascus!'* It had seventeen verses and a completely unmilitary tune; between verses we drank schnapps.

The soup cauldron in my back was beginning to simmer again, slowly filling up once more with liquid, and – I must admit – it was a pleasant, ticklish feeling.

Out with the goo, I thought, now it's all right for you to get well, as long as that lovely big hole makes you unfit for duty anyway.

Hubert was thrilled by the speed of the train. Standing in the open doorway he kept shouting: 'Hurry . . . hurry . . . all the way to Germany!'

I sat down beside him, dangling my legs and looking out at the smiling Hungarian countryside. It was terrific to see colourfully dressed people standing there sometimes and waving at us.

I had a long Virginia cheroot between my lips, it tasted deliciously bitter and mild, while in my back the goo of pus and blood and shreds of cloth and hand-grenade splinters went on simmering away.

'Mate,' the infantryman said to me, 'you shouldn't have thrown away your shirt.'

'What d'you mean?'

'The thing to do is wash it,' he said, 'wash it in cold water and flog it – they pay a lot here for underwear.'

'Have you been here before?'

He nodded, drew on his pipe, and puffed out the smoke.

'Yes,' he replied, 'I've been here before, the last time I was wounded, you can buy anything you like here. All you need is *pengö*. And the only way to get hold of *pengö* is by flogging. They've plenty to eat and drink, but they're always on the look-out for underwear and shoes.'

He drew again on his pipe.

'Yes,' he went on, 'for a shirt like that, if it'd been washed, you'd have had no trouble getting twenty or thirty *pengö*, and that means at least two bottles of schnapps – three hundred cigarettes – or three women . . .'

'Women, too?'

'That's right,' he said, 'women are expensive here because they're scarce. In the street you won't find any at all.' He suddenly perked up, looked out and, leaning forward, said: 'What the devil! We're stopping.'

So we were. Waiting on the ramp of the freight platform were lorries marked with red crosses. Hubert had come right up close to me. 'Now,' he said under his breath, 'it's now or never.'

A sergeant was already running along the platform, shouting: 'Everybody out! Everybody out, you're being unloaded here!'

'Oh shit,' said the fat infantryman, 'we're hardly out of Romania. This place is right close to Kronstadt.'

'D'you know it?' someone called out.

'Sure I do,' he said, 'it's called Siebenheiligegeorge. It used to be Romanian. Piss, I thought we'd be a bit nearer home by now.'

We all got out and stood on the platform until the doctor

came. As each man filed past him he scribbled something on the casualty slip.

'That means either hospital or casualty assembly point,' said the fat infantryman.

Hubert stood in front of me in the queue. When it was our turn the doctor glanced up.

'You're moving on,' he told Hubert. 'There's no point in leaving you back here with a wound like that. He'll take the place of the double amputee we've unloaded here,' he instructed the sergeant.

'He's got to move on too,' said Hubert, pointing at me.

'How's that?'

'He's my mate,' said the corporal. 'We've spent seventeen assault days and twenty-five close-combat days side by side in the shit, and the lad has a huge hole in his back.'

The doctor looked at me, and I thought: This is curtains, they're going to unload you here, and the whole mess wasn't worth the effort, you've no more money, can't buy any more booze, and it'll all heal up in no time. Then after two months you'll be up at the front again in some hole, and who knows whether you'll be that lucky next time.

'Hm,' went the doctor, his eyes still on me. 'Very well then, this man will take the place of the severe abdominal wound – got that?'

The sergeant nodded and indicated where we were to board the train.

I had no other luggage than my hands in my pockets, and it was glorious to saunter over to the train, but I must admit I was too ashamed to look back to where the others were being loaded onto lorries and driven into town.

'Wait a moment,' said Hubert as I was about to climb aboard. 'There's one catch to it – now we have to stay in bed

99

and won't be able to get hold of any booze. Come with me . . .'

We walked back across the rails and entered the station bar from the platform. The bar was deserted except for a few empty beer glasses and a lot of flies and heat and the reek of tepid food. He went over and tapped on the zinc counter top.

'Hallo!' he cried. 'Anybody at home?'

I had crossed the room and stood looking out into the street. It was a very broad, dusty road; on either side were flat-roofed houses under small, old trees.

All was silent and empty, until suddenly one of the lorries came dashing into the street, making the dust rise in a spreading cloud. The dust covered the whole sky, enveloped the little church spire . . . I turned away.

Hubert was standing at the counter negotiating with a neat, elderly woman who couldn't understand a word. They were both laughing. The woman reached under the counter and placed a bottle on it; moving closer I saw that it was a real cherry brandy.

'More,' said Hubert with a gesture. Out came the next bottle, apparently some kind of apricot brandy, then some real Scotch whisky.

After lining up six bottles in front of us, the woman wrote a figure with chalk on the kitchen door-frame, then made a quick addition and showed us the total: a hundred and ninety-two *pengö*. Hubert paid with two hundred-*pengö* notes.

'Christ,' I asked, 'how did you get hold of all that money?'

'God knows!' he said with a laugh. 'Maybe it was lying around in the street and I picked it up!'

Inside the hospital train everything looked so superior that I felt like a criminal. White beds and a nice, gentle nurse and background music from a radio.

We each lay on an upper bunk, close enough together for Hubert to be able to pass me the bottle.

'Just to make sure it doesn't heal up,' he said. 'Cheers!' We drank . . . In the bunk below me lay a man who'd had a bullet through his thigh bone; below Hubert lay a man whose left arm had been amputated. We shared our bottle with them. After two cherry brandies the man with the amputated arm grew quite talkative.

'Just imagine,' he said, 'my arm had been cut right through, like with a knife. A splinter must have sliced its way through, but the arm wasn't quite off. It still hung by a tendon, and I didn't feel a thing. I jumped up, the lieutenant helped me out of the trench, and I ran to the doctor with my arm dangling – you know, like those little balls you used to be able to buy at a fair, and there was masses of blood, but I ran as fast as I could. The doctor went "snip" with his scissors, just "snip", the way a barber snips off a single hair – and there lay my arm.' He laughed. 'I sometimes wonder where they buried it – let's have another drink. The doctor tells me it was all quite straightforward, it would heal up perfectly . . .' He paused to drink . . . 'Want another one too?' he asked the fellow lying beneath me.

'No, I don't think it's good for me. I feel sick.'

'Seems to me,' the one-armed man went on, 'I ought to get the gold badge now. What d'you think? I spent three weeks at the front and right the first day I got a graze and lost some blood – that counts, doesn't it? But I had to stay at the front, and a week later I caught another one, on my leg . . . I lost some more blood, so that's two wounds, right? And now this one, that makes three, so it seems to me they have to give me the gold, eh? Let's have the bottle again. My sergeant in the Reserve won't believe his eyes when I rejoin his unit with the gold badge plus the Iron Cross – after four weeks the gold plus the Iron Cross, for after all they're bound to give me the Iron Cross, too.' He laughed. 'He won't believe his eyes and he'll keep his mouth shut – he always said I was a slob, a great big slob, that I was the worst slob he'd ever known. He won't believe his eyes, will he!'

The windows had been blacked out, but you could hear the noise from the platform, and when I pushed aside the blind a bit there it actually was, a big platform.

'See anything?' asked the one-armed man. 'On this side there's only rails and freight cars.'

'Yes,' I said, 'a platform, and officers, and Hungarians and Germans, and women – it's dark . . . a few men are being carried out on stretchers.'

'What's the station called?' asked Hubert.

First I took a swig from the bottle, then looked for the sign: it must be somewhere along the platform, but I couldn't find it.

The nurse and an orderly came in, bringing sandwiches and cocoa. The man with the bullet through his thigh began groaning loudly. 'Shit!' he shouted at the nurse. 'I don't want to be fed – get that filthy metal out of my leg! Shit on your food, shit on your cocoa, I don't want any cocoa, any more than I wanted that metal in my leg!'

The nurse had turned pale. 'But,' she whispered, 'it's not my fault – wait a moment.' She put down the tray on a chair and hurried to the middle of the car, to a small white table with medication on it. There was now complete silence: everyone was listening to the thigh casualty's curses.

'Cocoa!' he swore, 'cocoa . . . so they think I'd go overboard with joy because I'm lying here in a white bed and get to drink cocoa! I've never wanted cocoa or this rocking-chair, and I never wanted any metal in my leg – I wanted to stay home, it's all shit, everything is shit . . . !' By this time he was yelling as if he'd gone out of his mind.

The nurse returned with a syringe.

'Give me a hand,' she said to the orderly, who was standing, silent and stupid, beside my bed.

The nurse looked at the temperature chart. 'Grolius,' she said in a low voice, 'do try and be reasonable. You're in pain, aren't you? I . . .'

'. . . An injection!' he yelled. 'What else, an injection! But . . .' he suddenly groaned, 'don't think I'm going to keel over with joy just because you're gracious enough to give me an injection . . . give the Führer an injection!'

You could have heard a pin drop. A voice said: 'For God's sake, give that arsehole an injection!'

No one spoke, and the nurse murmured: 'He's beside himself . . . really, he's beside himself . . .'

'Shit,' murmured the wounded man, and once more he whispered: 'Shit . . .' I leaned down and saw that he'd fallen asleep. His slack mouth looked bitter and almost black in the reddish stubble of his beard.

'There now!' the nurse said brightly. 'Now we'll have supper!'

She began handing round cocoa and sandwiches. The portion for the thigh casualty was placed on the one-armed man's chair. The cocoa was really good, and the sandwiches were spread with tinned fish.

After taking care of everyone, the nurse stood in the doorway holding the empty tray. 'Anyone else need anything . . . anything urgent?' she asked.

'Pills!' shouted someone from the far end of the car. 'Pills! I can't stand the pain!'

'What?' said the nurse. 'No, not now, in half an hour

you'll all be getting pills for the night anyway.'

'Nurse dear,' asked Hubert, 'where are we here?'

'We're in Nagykaroky,' she replied.

'Shit!' Hubert cried. 'Oh, goddamn shit!'

'What's matter?' I asked.

'Because we'll only be going as far as Debrecen after all. Half a night more at the most. Then there'll be another fucking hospital where we won't be allowed out.'

'But I thought we were going to Vienna, that's what I heard,' said the one-armed man. 'Aren't we?'

'Balls,' someone shouted. 'The train's going to Dresden.'

'Nonsense . . . Vienna Woods . . .'

'You'll see, Debrecen's the end of the line.'

'Really?' I asked.

'Are you sure?' I asked.

'Yes,' he said gloomily. 'Here, have a drink, I'm quite sure.'

But I didn't want a drink on top of the cocoa, I didn't want to destroy that wonderful sense of well-being. I smoked a cigarette, lay back carefully on my pillows and looked out into the night. I had tucked the blackout curtain slightly to one side and could look into the soft, dark grey night passing by. The train was moving again, everything was quiet except for the groans of the sleeping thigh casualty. Let's hope he sleeps all the way to Debrecen, I thought, let's hope the one-armed fellow keeps his mouth shut about his gold badge and his bloody sarge . . . and let's hope no one at either end of the car starts yelling and screaming 'shit'; and when the nurse comes I'll ask her to take my pulse so I can feel her gentle hand, and if she has some pills for me I'll let her put them into my mouth, like yesterday, and for a tenth of a second I'll feel her warm, white fingers on my lips.

But after the orderly had collected the dishes, they started playing gramophone records, Beethoven, and that made me cry, simply made me cry, because it reminded me of my mother.

Hell, I thought, never mind, no one's going to see. It was almost dark in the compartment, and we were being rocked from side to side, and I was crying . . . I would soon be nineteen, and I'd already been wounded three times, was already a hero, and I was crying because I was reminded of my mother.

In my mind's eye I clearly saw our home in Severin-Strasse, the way it had been before any bombs had fallen. A comfortable living room, very snug and warm and cheerful, and the street full of people, but no one knew who they were or why they were there. My mother was holding my arm, and we were silent, it was a summer evening and we were coming out of a concert . . . and my mother said nothing when I suddenly lit a cigarette, although I was only fifteen. There were soldiers in the street too, since it was war and yet not war. We weren't in the least hungry and not at all tired, and when we got home we might even drink a bottle of wine that Alfred had brought from France. I was fifteen and I would never have to be a soldier. And everything about Severin-Strasse felt so good. Beethoven, what a treat a Beethoven concert was.

I could see it all quite clearly. We had passed St Georg's, and a few whores had been standing there in the dark beside the urinal. Now we were passing the charming little square facing St Johann's, the small Romanesque church . . .

The street narrowed. We had to walk in the road and sometimes step aside for the tram; then we passed Tietz's, and finally the street widened out: there stood the great bulk of St Severin's tower. I could see everything so clearly: the shops with their displays – cigarettes, chocolate, kitchen spoons and leather soles. I could see it all as clear as day.

It was the nurse's gentle hand that startled me.

'Here we are,' came her voice, 'here's the Novalgin Quinine for your fever, and there,' she said as she handed me the thermometer, 'let's have your temperature!'

The mild fever gave me a feeling of contentment. It brought the goo on my back to the boil again, and now I was a hero again, four years older than before, wounded three times, and now an authentic, official hero. Even the sergeant in the Reserve wouldn't be able to touch me, for by the time I was back there again I would have the silver badge, so how could they possibly get at me . . . ?

By now I really did have a fever: 38.6, and the nurse entered a blue stroke on the curve of my chart that made it look quite alarming.

I had a fever, and from Debrecen it wasn't that far to Vienna, and from Vienna . . .

Maybe the front would collapse again at some corner, and there would be a big push, and we would all be moved to the rear, the way I'd heard it told so often – and like a shot we'd be in Vienna or Dresden, and from Dresden . . .

'Are you asleep, young fellow?' Hubert asked, 'or would you like another drink?'

'No,' I said, 'I'm asleep, asleep . . .'

'Okay, then. Goodnight.'

'Goodnight.'

But sleep was still a long way off. Somewhere towards the front of the car a man started screaming his head off. Lights were switched on . . . people shouted, ran, the nurse arrived and the doctor . . . and then all was quiet again.

The thigh casualty groaned and snored softly in his sleep . . .

Outside the night was once more totally dark, no longer grey; it was blue-black and silent, and I found I could no longer think of Severin-Strasse. I could think only of Debrecen . . . strange, I thought, when we did Hungary in geography you so often put your finger on Debrecen; it lay in the middle of a green patch, but not far away the colour turned to brown, then to very dark brown, that was the Carpathians, and who would ever have thought that one day you'd be swaying so quickly and quietly on your way to Debrecen, in the middle of the night. I tried to imagine the town.

Perhaps there would be some fine cafés there, and lots of things to buy, with *pengö* in your pocket. I glanced across at Hubert, but he had fallen asleep.

It was very quiet, and I longed for the tears to come again, but the image of my mother and of Severin-Strasse was completely wiped out.

The Cage

A man stood beside the fence looking pensively through the barbed-wire thicket. He was searching for something human, but all he saw was this tangle, this horribly systematic tangle of wires – then some scarecrow figures staggering through the heat towards the latrines, bare ground and tents, more wire, more scarecrow figures, bare ground and tents stretching away to infinity. At some point there was said to be no more wire, but he couldn't believe it. Equally inhuman was the immaculate, burning, impassive face of the blanched blue sky, where somewhere the sun floated just as pitilessly. The whole world was reduced to motionless scorching heat, held in like the breath of an animal under the spell of noon. The heat weighed on him like some appalling tower of naked fire that seemed to grow and grow and grow . . .

His eyes met nothing human; and behind him – he could see it even more clearly, without turning round – was sheer horror. There they lay, those others, round the inviolable football field, packed side by side like rotting fish; next came the meticulously clean latrines, and somewhere a long way behind him was also paradise: the shady, empty tents, guarded by well-fed policemen . . .

How quiet it was, how hot!

He suddenly lowered his head, as if his neck were breaking under the fiery hammer-blow, and he saw something that delighted him: the delicate shadows of the barbed wire on the bare ground. They were like the fine tracery of intertwining branches, frail and beautiful, and it seemed to him that they must be infinitely cool, those delicate tracings, all linked with each other; yes, they seemed to be smiling, quietly and soothingly.

He bent down and carefully reached between the wires to pick one of the pretty branches; holding it up to his face he smiled, as if a fan had been gently waved in front of him. Then he reached out with both hands to gather up those sweet shadows. He looked left and right into the thicket, and the quiet happiness in his eyes faded: a wild surge of desire flared up, for there he saw innumerable little tracings which when gathered up must offer a precious, cool eternity of shadow. His pupils dilated as if about to burst out of the prison of his eyeballs: with a shrill cry he plunged into the thicket, and the more he became entangled in the pitiless little barbs the more wildly he flailed, like a fly in a spider's web, while with his hands he tried to grasp the exquisite shadow branches. His flailings were already stilled by the time the well-fed policemen arrived to free him with their wire-cutters.

I Can't Forget Her

I can't forget her; whenever I emerge even for a moment from the vortex of everyday life which with its constant pressure tries to keep me beneath the surface of human reality; whenever I can even for a second turn my back on the ceaseless bustle of the crass pomposity they call life, and pause where their inane shouting cannot reach me: then her image appears before me, as close and distinct and ravishingly beautiful as I saw her years ago, when she was wearing a collarless coat that revealed all of her delicate neck.

At the time they had given up hope for me. The captain had said we were to make a counter-attack, and the lieutenant had made a counter-attack with us. But there was nothing to attack. We ran blindly up a wooded hill one spring evening, but on the expected battleground there was complete silence. We paused on the hill, looked away into the distance, and could see nothing. Then we ran down into the valley, up another hill, and paused again. There was not an enemy in sight. Here and there behind bushes were abandoned holes, half-finished positions of our troops in which the meaningless junk of war had been hastily left behind. It was still quiet; an uncanny silence lay heavily under the great vault of the spring sky that was slowly covering itself with the darker veils of twilight. It was so quiet that the lieutenant's voice startled us: 'Carry on!' he ordered. But as we were about to proceed the sky suddenly roared down upon us, and the earth burst open.

The others had quickly dropped to the ground or flung themselves into the abandoned holes; I just caught sight of the sergeant's pipe falling from his mouth, and then it felt as though they had knocked my legs from under my body . . .

Five men ran away after the first load had come down. Only the lieutenant and two men stayed behind; they hastily picked me up and ran down the slope with me while up above, where we had been lying, a fresh load came roaring down.

It was only much later, when all was quiet again and they laid me on the forest floor, that I felt any pain. The lieutenant wiped the sweat off his face and looked at me, but I could clearly see that he was not looking at the place where my legs must be. 'Don't worry,' he said, 'we'll get you back all right.'

The lieutenant placed a lighted cigarette between my lips, and I can still remember: while the pain increased again I still felt that life was beautiful. I was lying at the bottom of the valley on a forest path beside a little stream; up above, between the tall fir trees, only a narrow strip of sky was visible, a strip that was now silvery, almost white. The birds were singing, and an indescribably soothing silence reigned. I blew the cigarette smoke upward in long blue threads and felt that life was beautiful, and tears came to my eyes . . .

'It's all right,' said the lieutenant.

They carried me away. But it was a long way, almost two kilometres to the point where the captain had retreated, and I was heavy. I believe all wounded are heavy. The lieutenant carried the front end of the stretcher, and the other two walked behind. We slowly came out of the forest, across meadows and fields, and through another forest, and they had to set me down and wipe off their sweat, while the evening sank lower and lower. When we reached the village, everything was still quiet. They took me into a room where the captain now was. On both sides, school desks had been piled up against the walls, and the teacher's desk was covered with hand grenades. As I was being carried in, they were busy distributing the hand grenades. The captain was shouting into a telephone, threatening someone that he would have him shot. Then he let out a curse and hung up. They set me down behind the teacher's desk, where some other wounded were also lying. One of them was sitting there with his hand shot to pieces; he looked very contented.

The lieutenant gave a report on the counter-attack to the captain, and the captain yelled at the lieutenant that he would have him shot, and the lieutenant said, 'Yessir.' That made the captain yell even more, and the lieutenant again said, 'Yessir,' and the captain stopped yelling. They stuck big torches in flowerpots and lit them. By now it was dark, and there seemed to be no electric current. After the hand grenades had been distributed, the room emptied. All that was left were two sergeants, a clerk, the lieutenant and the captain. The captain said to the lieutenant: 'See that security sentries are placed all round the village; we'll try to get a few hours' sleep. Tomorrow we'll be starting out early.'

'To the rear?' asked the lieutenant quietly.

'Get out!' yelled the captain; the lieutenant left. After he had gone, I looked for the first time at my legs and saw that they were covered with blood, and I couldn't feel them, I felt only pain where normally I would have felt my legs. I was shivering now. Beside me lay a man who must have been shot in the stomach; he was very quiet and pale and scarcely moved; from time to time he merely stroked his hand, very quietly and carefully, across the blanket that covered his stomach. No one paid any attention to us. I imagine the medic had been among the five who had run away.

Suddenly the pain reached my stomach and crept higher very quickly; it flowed up like molten lead as far as my heart, and I believe I began to scream and then fainted . . .

I woke up and first heard music. I was lying on my side, looking into the face of the fellow with the stomach wound and saw that he was dead. His blanket was all black with congealed blood. And I could hear music, somewhere they must have found a radio. They were playing something quite modern, it must have been a foreign station; then the music was wiped out as if by a wet rag, and they played military marches, then came something classical, and they let that music go on. Then a voice above me said very softly, 'Mozart,' and I looked up and saw her face and realized at the same moment that it couldn't be Mozart, and I said to that face: 'No, it's not Mozart.'

She bent over me, and now I saw that she was a doctor or a medical student, she looked so young, but she was holding a stethoscope. Now all I could see was her loose, soft crown of brown hair, for she was bending over my legs, lifting the blanket so that I couldn't see anything. Then she raised her head, looked at me, and said: 'It *is* Mozart.' She pushed up my sleeve, and I said softly: 'No, it can't possibly be Mozart.'

The music went on playing, and now I was quite sure that it could never be Mozart. Some of it sounded like real Mozart, but there were other passages that couldn't possibly be Mozart.

My arm was all white. With gentle fingers she felt my pulse, then came a sudden needle prick, and she injected something into my arm.

As she did so, her head came quite close, and I whispered: 'Give me a kiss.' She blushed deeply, withdrew the needle, and at that moment a voice on the radio said:

113

'Dittersdorf.' Suddenly she smiled, and I smiled too, for now I could get a proper look at her because the only torch that was still burning was behind her. 'Quick,' I said in a louder voice, 'give me a kiss.' She blushed again and looked even more beautiful; the light from the torch shone on the ceiling and spread in wavering red circles round the walls. She gave a quick glance over her shoulder, then bent over me and kissed me, and at that instant I saw her closed eyelids from very near and felt those soft lips while the torch flung its restless light round the room and the captain's voice bellowed into the telephone again and now some different music was being spewed out of the speaker. Then a voice called out an order, someone picked me up and carried me out into the night and placed me in a cold van, and I had a last glimpse of her standing there, her eyes following me in the torchlight, right among all the school desks that were piled up like the absurd rubble of a collapsing world.

As far as I know, they are all back now in their proper jobs: the captain is an athletics instructor, the lieutenant is dead, and there's nothing I can tell you about the others – after all, I knew them only for a few hours. No doubt the school desks are back in their proper places, the electric light is working again, and torches are lit only on very romantic occasions; and instead of bellowing 'I'll have you shot!' the captain is now shouting something harmless such as perhaps: 'Idiot!' or 'Coward!', when someone can't do a grand circle on the crossbar. My legs have healed up, and I can walk quite well, and they tell me at the Veterans Affairs office that I should be working. But I have a different, much more important occupation: I am looking for her. I can't forget her. People tell me I'm crazy because I make no effort to do a grand circle in the air and land smartly on my feet like a good citizen and then, eager and thirsting for praise, step back in line.

Fortunately they are obliged to give me a pension, and I can afford to wait and search, for I know that I shall find her . . .

Green are the Meadows

The tram was crossing a street whose name – white on blue at the corner under the street-lamp – suddenly seemed familiar to him. He blushed, pulled out his notebook, and found the name of the street, circled in red, on a scribbled page: Bülow-Strasse. He now realized he had always passed over this page, although at heart he hadn't forgotten the name for so much as a single day . . .

The tram slowly rounded a curve and stopped. He heard music from a bar, saw gas lamps burning in the dusk; from somewhere beyond a garden fence came the laughter of young girls, and he got off. The suburb was like all the suburbs: pockmarked, dirty, dotted with little gardens and somehow appealing: it had the smell, the sound, the colour and the quite indescribable atmosphere of vulnerability . . .

The man heard the tram screeching off and set down his bundle. Although he knew the number by heart, he put his hand into his pocket and once more leafed through his notebook: 14 Bülow-Strasse. Now there was no way of avoiding it. He realized why he had always refused the job of picking up the cigarettes in this particular town. Of course there was many a Bülow-Strasse, every decent town had its Bülow-Strasse, but only in this town was there this house, number 14, where a woman by the name of Gärtner was living, a woman for whom he had a message about something that had happened four years ago and that he should have told her about four years ago . . .

The gas lamps lit up the high fence of a lumber yard, and

painted on the fence were huge white letters. Through the gaps he saw the light-coloured piles of trim boards, and he wearily deciphered the inscription on the fence: SCHUSTER BROTHERS: then he took a step backwards because the lettering on the fence was so big that his eyes had trouble following it, and much farther along, lit up by another gas lamp, he read: OLDEST LUMBER YARD IN TOWN. At the spot where he could read the final N of this display of integrity there was a large black house in which a few windows shone with a yellow light. The windows were open, he saw lamplight, heard radio music, and somewhere he heard again the girls' bright laughter. Someone was playing a guitar, and a few boys' voices were gently singing, 'We lay by the camp fire, Conchita and I . . .', other voices joined in, and a second guitar was struck up; the girls' laughter had died away.

The man walked slowly along beside the fence as far as the second gas lamp, which stood exactly between the T and the O. The shining tram rails continued on into a narrow street with closely packed buildings whose façades were almost dead, dark and frightening; the buildings seemed to have been burned out.

The dusk had grown thicker; he now saw those dead façades lit up by a tall, gently swaying lamp, and at the far corner there was another group of young fellows; the tips of their cigarettes glowed in the dusk. That must be the entrance to Bülow-Strasse . . .

He was still standing between the T and the O. It was quiet, with only the low, plaintive sounds of the two guitars and the soft voices coming to the end of the song. On the other side of the street were allotment gardens. Just then, a man standing in the dark lit his pipe, and he saw the match light up a fisherman's cap and a pudgy, heavy face, its lips puckered to blow out the match with one puff of smoke. Then all was swallowed up again in the silent darkness. He strolled slowly on, and at the end of the lumber yard's long fence the silence was suddenly broken; from the open doors of a bar came loud male laughter and in the background a frantic male voice yelling from a radio. The first cross-street seemed almost undamaged: loud laughter reached him and shouts and the murmuring conversation of people sitting on chairs outside their doors . . .

While walking past this scene as if he were passing an open, crowded living room, he was thinking: I can still go back. I don't have to be in this Bülow-Strasse. But he went on, as if under some compulsion, towards the traffic lights, and he had soon reached the group of young fellows at the street corner. There was some noise coming from Bülow-Strasse, too, but as he quickly turned the corner he saw that these façades also showed great black gaps, and for a moment he wished that number 14 might also have been destroyed. That would solve everything.

At the corner he hesitated. Once I enter the street, there's no going back, he thought. They will recognize me as a stranger, ply me with questions, and I'll have to tell them everything. He made a quick turn to the left and pushed his way through the group of youngsters into the bar. 'Evening all,' he said, sitting down at the table nearest the door. The landlord behind the counter, tall, thin, dark-complexioned, nodded and called out: 'Beer?'

'Yes,' said the man.

On a table to his right lay the crutches of an amputee. Beside the fat amputee, who had pushed his hat to the back of his head, sat a man and a woman with troubled expressions, their hands clasped wearily round their beer glasses. Over in a corner some men were playing cards, and

on the radio a woman was now singing, 'Mamma says it's
wrong to kiss, Mamma says it isn't done . . .' The landlord
brought the beer, and the man said, 'Thanks.' He put his
bundle down on the chair beside him and fumbled in his
breast pocket for a crumpled cigarette.

So this is it, he thought, this is the bar. This is where he
sang his 'Rosemarie' and his 'Green are the Meadows';
where he cursed yet proudly showed off his decorations,
where he bought cigarettes and stood singing at the
counter.

Then all he could see was the man, whose name had been
Gärtner, being shot to death by a sergeant called Stevenson.
That little, red-haired Stevenson with the cheeky face had
shot him right in the stomach with his machine pistol, four
shots one above the other, and he had never seen a mouth
that had once sung 'Rosemarie' so distorted with pain. They
had dragged him round the corner of a building, taken off
his tunic and ripped open his trousers; a mass of blood and
faeces had welled out of his stomach, and the mouth that
had once sung 'Rosemarie' and 'Green are the Meadows' in
this very bar had been silenced by pain. They had heard no
more shooting, they had taken his paybook from his pocket,
and he had jotted down: Gärtner, 14 Bülow-Strasse, with
the idea of telling the wife if he should ever find himself in
this town. Gärtner hadn't said another word, that horrible
mass of blood and faeces came slowly welling out of his
stomach, and they – the other man and himself – could only
look on helplessly until suddenly a voice behind them
shouted 'Hands up!' and they discovered that this red-
haired sergeant was called Stevenson. The next moment
twelve trembling Americans were standing round them,
and he had never seen men tremble like that; they trembled
so much that he could hear the light tinkling of their

machine pistols, and one of the Americans said: 'That's one gone, Stevenson . . .'

Stevenson made a swift, discarding gesture; he and the other man understood and threw their weapons behind them. The other man – he had never found out his name, they had only known each other for half an hour – had been carrying a machine gun like a big black cat under his arm; now he flung the machine gun behind him into a broad puddle of wet ordure. He heard it splash, just as in the old days their swimming instructor had demonstrated a dive, and in his mind's eye he could still see the bald, yellow globe of the gas lamp. He only came to when one of the Americans in his excitement fired a shot right past his nose, and they saw that Gärtner was dead and heard tanks rumbling towards them . . .

He looked at his beer and noticed a little vase of flowers next to his glass – a twig with yellow, plump, but fading pussy-willow, and he realized that spring had come round again, just as it had done so long ago. It must be exactly four years since Stevenson had shot Gärtner in the stomach until blood and faeces poured out. The amputee gave a brutal shrug, and the expressions of the man and woman became still more troubled. The youths outside the door must now have been joined by the girls: he could hear the girls' high laughter, and then they all began to sing, and the man and woman sitting with the fat amputee, their hands still miserably clasping their beer glasses, now looked through the open door and listened to the singing. 'Max!' the amputee called out to the landlord. 'Bring us three more beers, will you?'

The man could hear that the couple sitting with the amputee were trying to whisper their objections. Outside the young people were singing songs whose words he couldn't make out, soft, soothing, sentimental tunes.

The landlord came past his table, picked up the empty glass, and asked: 'Same again?'

'Yes.'

The man glanced at the cigarettes he had wrapped in a pair of blue work trousers. Outside the laughing, singing voices of the boys and girls gradually moved away. From the radio now came a talk, and the landlord twiddled the knobs doggedly until music came on again.

'I'd like to pay!' the man called out.

The landlord came over. While putting down the money he asked in a low voice: 'Gärtner – didn't Gärtner use to come here quite often?'

'That's right,' the landlord said at once, smoothing out the note the man had given him. 'Did you know him? Willi Gärtner?'

'Yes. Is he still alive?'

'No, he got killed in the war.'

'When?'

'Oh, I don't know – quite late, I think, towards the end. Where did you meet him?'

'We worked together.'

'At Plattke's?'

'Yes, at Plattke's . . . and his wife, what's she doing?'

The landlord looked at him in surprise: 'But she's at Plattke's now! Aren't you there any more?'

'No, I'm not . . .'

'I see,' said the landlord indifferently. He picked up the empty glass and called out to another customer: 'Just a moment – I'm coming!'

The man got up, quietly said, 'Goodnight,' and, without looking back, left the bar.

Here and there in the unlit, open windows he could see

the glow of cigarettes, and he could hear the distant wail of radio sets. The building next door to the bar was number 28. It was a grocery. In the dim half-light he could see the cardboard signs for Maggi and Persil, and in the gloom beyond the shop window a basket of eggs, a pile of cereal packages, and a big glass jar with sour pickles and onions floating around in it. It was like looking through the glass of a neglected aquarium. The objects seemed to float and sway, mollusc-like, slimy creatures carrying on their lecherous existence in the dim half-dark.

So this is it, he thought. This is where his wife bought her vinegar and soup packets and cigarettes, and somewhere round here there'll also be a butcher and a baker . . . a stomach like that must, after all, be nourished for a long time before it can be shot up so expertly that blood and faeces come pouring out in a viscous stream. Everything must be done in its proper order. For at least eighteen years a stomach like that must be regularly filled with all those things to be bought for a week's wages from the butcher, the baker and the grocer; and sometimes that stomach must also drink beer and sing, and the mouth belonging to that stomach is also allowed to smoke cigarettes, everything in its proper order . . .

The people sitting outside their doors have no idea that somewhere in the world there is an American who shot up their Willi – right through the stomach – flutch . . . flutch . . . flutch . . . flutch . . . he would never forget that sound, the demonic mildness, that gentle flopping which had riddled Gärtner's stomach.

The people didn't seem to notice him. He was just someone going home with a pair of blue work trousers under his arm. He stopped and fumbled in his breast pocket for another crumpled cigarette. The crumpled ones were his, that had been agreed. As he stood there he glanced at the next front door and saw that it was number 18. Then came a gap, so the next house must be number 14. He saw lighted windows there and some chairs outside the door.

Glowing ashes had been scattered all over the bomb site, and here and there the remains of briquets were smouldering and there was a smell of rags and potato peelings that had caught fire. In a lighted window he had a fleeting glimpse of a heavy, stout fellow with a cigar in his mouth, and behind his back a woman standing at a stove in front of a smoking frying pan.

Four years ago it had also been spring, it had also been April, everything had turned green again after a terrible winter. They had been aware of that in the chill nights when they had crouched futilely in their holes, guarding bridges over rivers that in many thousands of places could be waded across: they had been aware of it: it was spring. And when the grey dawn came they retreated, attacked and were attacked. The troop units were torn apart, patched together again. Whole regiments cleared out or went over to the enemy; many of the men were caught again at street corners and rounded up, and there was always some officer there to take command. They were posted at street corners or shoved at night into holes just so they could be well and truly shot to pieces. As a result one found oneself with new comrades every day. He had known Gärtner for only half an hour. A lieutenant had arrived and said, 'Come with me!' and had stationed him at the intersection beside Gärtner and the man with the machine gun. Gärtner had given him a cigarette, which at that time was worth more than all the decorations put together. Grenades had burst somewhere, tanks had rumbled, there had been some shooting, and

123

suddenly those bullets had flopped into Gärtner's stomach . . .

He was still staring at the glowing piles of ashes, breathing in the repulsive stench of scorched rags. Outside number 14 two women were sitting on chairs, dark, stoutish figures in whispered conversation. In the doorway itself stood a young fellow, smoking; he walked towards the youth and said: 'Could I have a light, please?'

In silence the fellow casually held his glowing butt against the cigarette, and while the kitchen odours that permeated the youth's clothing rose into the man's nostrils together with the smell of cheap soap, he looked beyond his cigarette into the open, unlit corridor, and then – in that half-second he needed for lighting his cigarette – he heard a couple embracing in there in the dark; he heard those indescribable sounds of wordless tenderness, that gentle groaning that was like suppressed pain; he felt the blood mounting, hot and tormenting, to his head. He hurriedly thanked the youth and walked quickly, very quickly, back, past the glowing ash heaps, past the un-damaged houses, the gaps and the grocery. By the time he reached the corner he was almost running because he could hear the tram screeching towards him from behind; and when he glanced over his shoulder and saw its dim yellow lights approaching in the gentle, spring darkness, he broke into a run.

He was so afraid of missing the tram that before reaching the tram stop, where he paused for a moment, he caught only snatches of the young people's singing: the group now seemed to be standing somewhere near the allotment gardens. Now they were singing 'Green are the Meadows' so earnestly and meltingly that no more laughter was to be heard between the verses.

The tram came to a stop and he was glad to be able to get on. He wiped away his sweat, had one more passing glimpse of the lumber yard's neatly lettered fence, and wished that the tram could have continued on and on, forever . . .

The Rain Gutter

For a long time they lay awake smoking while the wind swept through the house, loosening tiles and tumbling bricks; pieces of plaster sailed down with a crash from the upper floors, shattering below and spreading into rubble.

He saw only a dim sheen of her, a warm, reddish hue when they drew on their cigarettes: the soft outlines of her breasts under her nightgown and her calm profile. The sight of the narrow, firmly closed crease between her lips, that little valley in her face, filled him with tenderness. They tucked the covers in firmly at the sides, nestled close together, and knew that they would keep warm all night long. The shutters rattled, and the wind whistled through the jagged holes in the window panes; above them it howled in the remains of the attic, and somewhere there was the sound of an object slapping noisily and steadily against a wall, something hard, metallic, and she whispered: 'That's the gutter, it's been broken for a long time.'

She was silent for a moment, then took his hand and softly went on: 'The war hadn't started yet, and I was already living here, and whenever I came home I'd see the piece of gutter hanging there, and I'd think: they *must* have it repaired; but they never did. It hung crooked, one of the clamps had come loose, and it always seemed about to fall at any moment. I always heard it when there was a wind, every night when there was a storm and I was lying here. And when the war started it was still hanging there. On the grey house wall you could clearly see where the water had flowed sideways into the wall after every rain: a white path, with a grey border leading down past the window, and on either side there were big round patches with white centres surrounded by darker grey rings. Later on I went far away, I was put to work in Thuringia and Berlin, and when the war was over I came back here, and the gutter was still hanging there: half the building had collapsed – I'd been far away, far, far away, and I'd seen so much pain, death and blood, they had shot at me with machine guns from airplanes, and I'd been scared, so scared – and all that time that piece of galvanized iron had been hanging here, sending the rain into empty space because the wall below was almost completely gone. Roof tiles had fallen off, trees had been toppled, plaster had come crumbling down, bombs had fallen, so many bombs, but that piece of galvanized iron had continued to hang from that one clamp, it had never been hit, its crooked slant had never given way to the blasts.'

Her voice became even lower, almost a chant, and she pressed his hand. 'So much rain came raining down,' she said, 'in those six years, so many deaths were died, cathedrals destroyed, but the gutter was still hanging there when I came back. Once again I heard it clattering at night whenever there was a wind. Can you believe that I was happy?'

'I can,' he said.

The wind had subsided, it was quiet now, and the cold crept closer. They pulled up the covers and hid their hands inside. In the darkness he could no longer distinguish anything, he couldn't even see her profile, although she was lying so close that he could feel her breath, her calm, regular breathing warm against his skin, and he thought she had fallen asleep. But suddenly he could no longer hear her breathing and he groped for her hands. She moved her hand down and grasped his and held onto it, and he knew they would be warm and he wouldn't have to shiver all night long.

Suddenly he became aware that she was crying. There was nothing to be heard, he just knew from the movements of the bed that she was wiping her face with her left hand. Even that wasn't certain, but he knew she was crying. He sat up, bent over her and felt her breath again: it seemed to spread over his face like a current gently flowing past him. Even when his nose touched her cold cheek, he still could see nothing.

'Lie down,' she whispered, 'you'll catch cold.'

He remained leaning over her, he wanted to see her, but he saw nothing until she suddenly opened her eyes: then he saw the glint of her eyes in the darkness, the shimmering tears.

She cried for a long time. He took her hand, held it, and firmly tucked in the covers again. He held her hand for a long time, until her grip relaxed and her hand slowly slipped out of his – he put his arm round her shoulder, drew her close, and then he too fell asleep, and as they slept their breathing alternated like caresses . . .

Autumn Loneliness

How long we spent standing there at the corner I can't tell you. I was filled with a sense of anticipation that was really quite unjustified. It was now autumn, and each time a tram stopped at the corner people came streaming towards us, their footsteps rustling in the dead leaves, and in their steps was joy, the joy of people going home.

We must have stood there for a long time. It had been still quite light when suddenly, without a word, we had stopped, as if to mount guard over the deepening melancholy of autumn, a mood caught in the tops of the plane trees as they slowly shed their leaves.

There was no real reason for it, but each time the tram rang its bell at the corner and people came streaming into the avenue towards us and the tram drove on ringing its bell – each time I was convinced that someone was about to come, someone who knew us, who would ask us to join him, whose homeward steps would force our own weary, aimless footsteps to keep up with the tempo of his happy excitement.

The first ones always came singly and walked very fast; then came the groups, in twos or even threes in animated conversation, and finally another trickle of weary individuals passing us with their heavy burdens before dispersing into the houses scattered among gardens and avenues.

It was a constant suspense that held me spellbound, for after the last person had passed by there was only a brief respite before we heard the distant ping-pinging of the next tram at the previous stop – clanking and screeching its way to the corner.

We stood under the branches of an elderberry tree that reached out over the street far beyond the fence of a neglected garden. Rigid with tension, he had his face turned in the direction of the people approaching through the rustling leaves – the face which, mute and set, had been accompanying me for two months, which I had loved, and also hated, for two months . . .

During the time it took four trams to arrive, the tension and anticipation felt wonderful as we stood there in the steadily deepening melancholy of dusk, in the soft, exquisite, damp decay of autumn; but all of a sudden I knew that no one to whom I might belong would ever come . . .

'I'm leaving,' I said huskily, for I had been standing there much too long as if rooted to the bottom of some swampy bowl that was about to close imperceptibly over me with a velvety, relentless force.

'Go ahead,' he said without looking at me, and for the first time in two months he forgot to add: 'I'll come with you.'

His eyes narrowed to slits; without moving, he kept his hard, metallic gaze fixed on the deserted avenue where now only a few single leaves were slowly circling to the ground.

All right, I thought, and at that moment something happened to me, something was released, and I felt my face collapsing, felt sharp, bitter lines forming round my mouth. It was almost as if my inner tension had been tightly wound up and was now being released as if by a blow: uncoiling inside me with incredible speed, leaving nothing behind but that hollow, mournful void that had been there two months ago. For at that moment it dawned on me: he was standing here waiting for something quite specific; this spot, this street corner under the spreading branches of the elderberry tree, was his objective, the goal of an arduous flight, of a journey lasting two months, while for me it was just another street corner, one of many thousand.

I watched him for a long time, which I could do undisturbed as he had ceased to notice me. Perhaps he thought I had already left. In his watchful gaze was something resembling hate, while his shallow, rapid breathing shook him like the prelude to an explosion . . .

If only he would remember, I sighed to myself, to give me one of the two cigarettes and my share of the bread. I was afraid to ask, for now the tram was stopping again at the corner. Then I saw, very briefly, the first and last smile on his face before he rushed forward with a smothered cry. From among a cluster of people, some of whom he had thrust aside, I heard a woman's gasp breaking the melancholy silence of the autumnal evening, and something like a shadow fell across the astonished void of my heart, for now I knew that I would have to go on inexorably alone, that I would also have to accept the loss of the cigarette and the bread and of the two months of shared danger and shared hunger . . .

I turned away, dipped my tired feet into the golden waves of dead leaves and walked out of the town, once again towards that Somewhere. The freshness of the falling light was still permeated by the spicy smell of burning potato plants, the smell of childhood and of longing. The sky was starless and drained of colour. Only the grinning face of the moon hung over the horizon, watching me mockingly as I plodded on under the weight of the darkness, towards that Somewhere . . .

Beside the River

To tell the truth, I'd never known the meaning of despair. But then, a few days ago, I found out. All of a sudden the whole world seemed grey and wretched; nothing, nothing mattered any more, and I had a bitter lump in my throat, and I thought there was no way out for me, no escape and no help. For I had lost all our ration cards, and at the ration office they would never believe me, they wouldn't replace them, and we had no more money for the black market, and stealing – I really didn't like to steal, and anyway I couldn't steal enough for that many people. For Mother and Father, for Karl and Grete, and for myself, and for our youngest, the baby. And the special mother's card was gone, and Father's manual worker's card – everything, everything was gone, the whole briefcase. I suddenly realized it in the tram, and I didn't bother to look or even ask. It's useless, I thought – who's going to hand over ration cards, and so many, and the mother's card and Father's manual worker's card . . .

At that moment I knew the meaning of despair. I got off the tram much earlier and walked straight down to the Rhine; I'll drown myself, I thought. But when I reached the bare, cold avenue and saw the calm, wide, grey river it came to me that it's not so easy to drown oneself; still, I wanted to do it. It must take a long time to die, I thought, and I would have liked a quick, sudden death. Obviously I couldn't go home any more. Mother would simply throw up her hands, and Father would give me a good hiding and say it was a disgrace: a big lout like that, almost seventeen, who's no good for anything anyway, not even for the black market – a big lout like that goes and loses all the ration cards when

he's sent out to queue up for the fat rations! And I didn't
even get the fat. It was all gone after I had been queuing for
about three hours. Still, that might not have lasted too
long, that trouble with Father and Mother. But we would
have nothing to eat, no one would give us anything. At the
ration office they would laugh in our faces because once
before we had lost a few coupons; and as for selling or
flogging something, we had long ago run out of things,
and stealing – you can't steal for so many.

No, I had to drown myself, since I didn't have the nerve
to throw myself under some big fat American car. There
were many cars driving beside the Rhine, but there wasn't
a soul in the avenue. It was bare and cold, and a damp, icy
wind blew from the grey, swift-flowing water. I kept
walking straight ahead and eventually was surprised at
how fast I reached the end of the avenue. The trees seemed
to fall away on either side of me, keeling over like poles
and disappearing, and I didn't dare look back. So I very
quickly reached the end of the avenue where the Rhine
widens out a bit and there is a launching ramp for kayaks
and a little farther on the ruined bridge. There wasn't a
soul there either, only over by the launching ramp an
American sat staring into the water. It was odd, the way he
was crouching there, sitting on his heels; it was probably
too cold to sit on the stones, so there he squatted, throwing
precious cigarette butts into the water. Each butt, I
thought, is almost half a loaf of bread. Perhaps he isn't
smoking at all, but all the Americans just smoke a quarter
of a cigarette and throw the rest away. I know it for a fact.
He's lucky, I thought, he's not hungry and hasn't lost any
coupons, and with every butt he throws three marks and
seventy-five pfennigs into the cold grey Rhine. If I were
he, I thought, I'd sit down by the stove with a cup of coffee

instead of squatting here by the cold Rhine and staring into the dirty water . . .

I ran on; yes, I believe I did run. My thoughts about the American had been very brief and fleeting; I had envied him no end, it was terrible how I envied him. So I walked on or ran, I forget now, all the way to the ruined bridge, thinking: if you jump off from up there it's all over, all over in no time. I once read that it is hard to drown yourself by going into the water slowly. You have to plunge in from high up, that's the best way. So I ran towards the ruined bridge. There were no workmen there. Maybe they were on strike, or it's imposs- ible to work out there on the bridges in cold weather. I saw nothing more of the American, I never once looked back.

No, I thought, there's no help and no hope, and no one will replace our ration cards, there are too many of us, Father and Mother, my brother and sister, the baby and I, plus the special mother's card and Father's manual worker's card. It's hopeless, drown yourself, then at least there'll be one less mouth to feed. It was very, very cold, there in the avenue beside the Rhine; the wind whistled, and bare branches fell from the trees that in summertime are so beautiful.

It was difficult to climb onto the ruined bridge; they had knocked out what remained of the paving, and there was only the skeleton left, and along it ran a kind of little railway, probably for hauling away the rubble.

I climbed very carefully, and I was terribly cold and very much afraid of falling off. I can well remember thinking: how stupid to be scared of falling since you want to drown yourself! If you fall off here, onto the street or onto the rubble, you'll also be dead, and that'll be all right, that's what you want. But it's quite a different thing, I can't explain it. What I wanted was to throw myself into the water and not smash onto the ground, and I thought of all the pain one might suffer and maybe not even be dead. And I didn't want to suffer. So I climbed very carefully over the bare bridge right to the end, the very end where the rails stick out in the air. There I stood, looking into the grey, grey murmuring water, there I stood close to the very end. I felt no fear, only despair, and suddenly I knew that despair is beautiful, it is sweet and nothing, it is nothing, and nothing matters any more.

The Rhine was fairly high, and grey and cold, and for a long time I stared into its face. I also saw the American squatting there, and really did see him throw a precious butt into the water. I was surprised to find him so near, much nearer than I had thought. I looked once again along the whole length of the bare avenue, and then suddenly looked down into the Rhine again, and I became terribly dizzy, and then I fell! All I remember is that my last thought was of Mother, and that it might after all be worse for me to be dead than to have lost the ration cards, the whole lot . . . Father's and Mother's and my brother's and sister's and the baby's, plus the special mother's card and Father's manual worker's card, and . . . yes, yes, my card too, although I'm a useless mouth, no good even for the black market . . .

I guess I must have sat there for an hour beside the murky Rhine, staring into the water. All I could think of was that blonde broad, Gertrud, who was driving me nuts. Hell, I thought, spitting my cigarette into the Rhine: throw yourself in, into that grey brew, and let it carry you down to – to Holland, yes, and still farther, say into the Channel, right down to the bottom of the sea! There wasn't a soul around, and the water was driving me nuts. I know for sure it was the water, and my thinking all the time of that good-looking broad who wouldn't have me. Nope, she wouldn't have me, and I knew for sure that I'd never, never get anywhere with her. And the water wouldn't let go of me, the water was driving me nuts. Hell, I thought, throw yourself in and those goddamn women won't bother you any more, throw yourself in . . .

And then I heard someone running along the avenue like a maniac. I've never seen anyone run like that. He's in trouble, I thought, and stared at the water again, but the footsteps in the deserted avenue above made me look up again, and I saw the kid running toward the wrecked bridge, and I thought, I'll bet they're after him and I hope he gets away, never mind if he's been stealing or whatever. A thin, lanky kid, running like a maniac. Again I looked at the water – throw yourself in, a voice kept whispering . . . You'll never get her, never, throw yourself in and let the grey brew carry you to Holland, goddammit, and I spat the third cigarette into the water.

For God's sake, I thought, what are you doing here in this country, in this crazy country, where every living soul can think of nothing but cigarettes? In this crazy country where the bridges are all gone and there's no colour, no colour anywhere, dammit, only grey. And everyone chasing after God knows what. And that girl, that crazy, long-legged broad, will never be yours, not for a million cigarettes will she be yours, damn it to hell.

But just then I heard that crazy kid crawling around up there on the bridge. The iron skeleton rang hollow under his boots, and the crazy kid climbed right out to the far end, and there he stood, for the longest time, also looking into the dirty grey water, and all of a sudden I knew that no one was chasing him, but that he . . . Goddammit, I thought, he wants to throw himself into the water! And I got a real shock and couldn't take my eyes off the spot where that crazy kid was standing, not moving, not making a sound, up there in the gap of the ruined bridge, and he seemed to sway a little . . .

I automatically spat the fourth cigarette into the Rhine and I couldn't take my eyes off that figure up there. I turned cold all over, I was terrified. That boy, that young kid, what kind of troubles can he have, I thought? Girl trouble, and I laughed – at least I think I laughed, I can't be sure. Can this young kid already have girl trouble, I thought? The water said nothing, and it was so quiet that I thought I could hear that kid's breathing as he went on standing there, motionless, silent, in the gap of the ruined bridge. Goddammit, I thought, it mustn't happen, and I was just going to call out when I thought, you'll scare him and then he'll fall for sure. The silence was weird, and we two were all alone in the world with this dirty grey water.

And then, for God's sake, he looked at me, really looked at me, and I was still sitting there, not moving a muscle and Splash! the crazy kid was actually down there in the water!

That really woke me up, and in no time I'd thrown off my jacket and cap. I dived into the cold water and started swimming. It was hard work, but luckily the current carried him toward me. Then suddenly he was gone, gone under, dammit, and my shoes were full of water, they felt like lead on my feet, my shirt was like lead too, and it was cold, icy cold, and not a sign of the kid anywhere . . . I paddled on, then trod water for a bit and shouted, yes shouted . . . and dammit if the kid didn't come up again, he was already a bit downstream, and I hadn't thought the current was that fast. Now my body seemed to warm up a bit, with panic, at the sight of that lifeless bundle being swept off in that grey dirty water, and me after it, and when I was less than two yards away – I could actually see the blond hair – he was gone again, just gone, dammit . . . but I was after him, head down, and Christ Almighty! I'd grabbed hold of him.

Nobody in the world can know how relieved I was when I'd grabbed hold of him. In the middle of the Rhine, and there was only grey, cold, dirty water, and I was as heavy and cold as lead, and yet I felt relieved. It's just that I had no more fear, that's what it must have been . . . and I swam slowly across the current with him to the shore and was surprised at how close the shore was.

Jesus, I had no time to shiver or moan, although I'd had a lousy time of it. I'd swallowed a whole lot of water, and the dirty stuff made me feel sick as a dog, but I rested till I got my breath back, then I grabbed his arms and pumped them up and down, up and down, up and down, just like they tell you to, and I got pretty damn hot over it . . . There wasn't a living soul up there on the river bank, and no one heard it or saw it. Then the kid opened his eyes, a pair of bright blue child's eyes, for God's sake, and he sicked up water, kept sicking it up . . . Dammit, I thought, the kid's got nothing but water in his stomach, and nothing but water came up, and then he felt he had to smile, the kid actually smiled at me . . .

By that time I was as cold as hell in those wet things, and I thought, you'll catch your death, and he was shaking like a leaf too.

Then I pulled him up and said: 'Go on, boy . . . run!' and I just grabbed him by the arm and ran up the ramp with him, he was as limp as a rag doll in my arm, then he stopped again and sicked up some more grey water, dirty grey Rhine water, that was all, then he could run better.

Goddamn, I thought, he has to get warm and you have to get warm, and in the end we ran pretty good, right up to the avenue and then a bit along the avenue. I began to feel quite warm and I sure was panting, but the kid was still shaking like a leaf. Dammit, I thought, he needs to get indoors and then into a bed, but there were no houses there, just a few piles of rubble and some rails, and it was already getting dark. But then one of our vehicles turned up, a Jeep, and I dashed out onto the street and waved my arms. First it drove on, there was a black driving it, but I yelled at the top of my voice: 'Hey there, bud . . .' and he must have heard from my voice that I was an American – you see, I wasn't wearing a jacket or a cap. So he stopped, and I hauled the kid over, and the black shook his head and said: 'Poor kid – almost drowned, did he?'

'Yes,' I answered, 'let's go, and step on it!' I told him where my billet was.

The boy sat next to me and gave me another of those pathetic smiles, enough to make me feel pretty weird, and I felt his pulse a bit, it seemed okay.

'Hurry!' I shouted to the black. He turned around and grinned and really did speed up, and all the time I was saying: 'Make a left, now right, right again,' and so on till we actually stopped at my billet.

Pat and Freddie were standing in the hallway and laughed when they saw me coming: 'Boy oh boy, is that your charming Gertrud?' But I told them: 'Don't laugh, fellows, help me, I've just fished this kid here out of the Rhine.' They helped me carry him upstairs to our room, Pat's and my room, and I told Freddie: 'Make us some coffee.' Then I threw him down on the bed, pulled off his wet things, and rubbed him for a long time with my towel. God, how skinny the kid was, how terribly skinny . . . he looked like . . . like, hell, like a long, limp, white noodle.

'Pat,' I said, for Pat was standing there watching me, 'you go on rubbing, I have to get out of these wet things.' I was as

139

wet as a drowned rat, too, and scared to death of getting the flu. Then Pat handed me the towel, for the lanky kid on the bed was now red all over like a baby, and he smiled again . . . and Pat felt his pulse and said: 'Okay, Johnny, he's going to be all right, I guess.'

The boys were damn good about it; Freddie brought us some coffee, and Pat scrounged some underwear for the kid, who lay on the bed drinking coffee and smiling, and Pat and I sat on the chairs, and Freddie went off, I guess he went off to the girls again.

Jesus, I thought, what a scramble, but it turned out okay, thank God!

Pat stuck a cigarette between the kid's lips, and you should've seen how he smoked! These Germans, I thought, they all smoke like crazy, they suck on those things as if they contained life itself, their faces go all queer. And then I remembered that my jacket was still lying down there by the water, with the photo, and my cap too, but shit, I thought, why would I still need that photo . . .

It was real peaceful and quiet, and the kid was happily chewing away, for Pat had given him some more bread and a can of corned beef and kept refilling his mug with coffee.

'Pat,' I said after a while as I lit up too. 'Pat, d'you suppose it's all right to ask him why he tried to drown himself?'

'Sure,' Pat replied, and asked him.

The lad gave us a wild look and said something to me, and I looked at Pat and Pat shrugged his shoulders. 'He's saying something about food, but there's one word I can't understand, I just don't get it . . .'

'What word?' I asked.

'*Marken*,' Pat said.

'*Marken*?' I asked the boy.

He nodded and said another word, and Pat said: 'He's lost them – those things, those *Marken* . . .'

'What's that, *Marken*?' I asked Pat. But Pat didn't know.

'*Marken*,' I said to the boy. '*Was ist das*?' – that being one phrase I could say properly in German, and I could say *Liebe* too, that's all. That goddamn broad had taught me . . .

The boy looked baffled; then with his thin fingers he drew a funny kind of square on the top of the bedside table and said: '*Papier*.'

I can understand *Papier* too, and I thought I knew now what he was trying to say.

'Ah,' I said, 'pass, you've lost your pass!'

He shook his head: '*Marken*.'

'Damn it all, Pat,' I said, 'this *Marken* is driving me nuts. It must be something pretty special to make him want to drown himself.'

Pat refilled our mugs, but that damned *Marken* kept nagging at me. My God, hadn't I seen that youngster standing up there, not moving, not making a sound, in the gap of the ruined bridge, and Splash! goddammit?

'Pat,' I said, 'look it up, you've got a dictionary.'

'Sure,' said Pat, jumping up and bringing the dictionary from his locker.

Meanwhile I nodded at the boy and gave him another cigarette, he'd eaten the whole can of corned beef and all the bread, and the coffee must've done him a power of good. And Jesus, the way these guys smoke, it's crazy, they smoke the way we sometimes used to smoke in the war when things got tough. They always smoke as if it was war-time, these Germans.

'Here we are!' Pat cried. 'Got it!', and he jumped up, took a letter out of his locker, and showed the kid the stamp on it, but the boy just shook his head and even smiled a bit.

'*Nee,*' he said, and he repeated that crazy word that had made him try and drown himself, and I'd never heard it.

'Hold it,' Pat said, 'I've got it, it's a word that means "ration cards",' and he quickly turned over the pages of his dictionary.

'Still hungry?' I gestured to the kid. But he shook his head and poured himself another cup of coffee. Jesus, the way they can put away coffee, by the bucket, I thought . . .

'Damn it all,' Pat cried, 'these dictionaries, these crappy dictionaries, these goddamn fucking dictionaries – a kid like that tries to drown himself for some reason or other, and you can't even find it in the dictionary.'

'Look,' I said to the boy, in English of course, 'just tell us what it is, take your time, we're all human, we must be able to understand each other. Tell him, tell Pat,' and I pointed to Pat, 'just tell this guy.' And Pat laughed, but he listened very carefully and the boy told him slowly, very slowly, the poor kid was all embarrassed, taking his time about it, and I understood some of it, and Pat's expression turned very serious.

'I'll be damned!' Pat exclaimed. 'How can we be so dumb! They get their food on ration cards, right? They have ration cards, get it? Goddammit, we never thought of it, and that's what he's lost, and that's why he jumped into the Rhine.'

'I'll be damned,' I muttered. 'A kid like that jumps into the river, and we don't know why, can't imagine . . .'

We should at least be able to imagine it, I thought, at the very least, even if we can't actually experience it, we should at least be able to imagine it . . .

'Pat,' I said, 'if he's lost them, they'll have to give him

some new ones. It's just paper, and they can print them, they simply have to give him some new paper – it's not money, after all. It can happen to anyone, you know, losing them, surely there must be plenty of that printed stuff around . . .'

'Balls,' Pat replied, 'they'll never do it. Because there's some people who just *say* they've lost them, and they sell them or eat twice as much, and the authorities get fed up. Christ, it's like in the war, when you've lost your rifle and suddenly there's a guy coming at you, and you simply can't shoot because you haven't got a rifle. It's just a goddamn war they're carrying on with their paper, that's what it is.'

Okay, I thought, but that's terrible, then these folks end up having nothing to eat, nothing, nothing at all, and there's not a thing to be done about it, and that's why he ran like a maniac and threw himself into the Rhine . . .

'Yes,' Pat said, as if answering my thoughts, 'and he's lost them all, the whole lot, for – I believe it's six people, and some other cards too, I just don't get what he means – for a whole month . . .'

Jesus, I thought, what are they going to do if that's how it is! They can't do a thing, that kid goes and loses all the ration cards, and I thought to myself I'd drown myself too if I was him. But I still couldn't imagine it . . . no, I guess nobody can imagine it.

I stood up, went over to my locker and got two packs of cigarettes for the kid but then I really had a shock, the way he looked at me. He sure gave me a weird look, he's going to go out of his mind on us, I thought, clear out of his mind, that's the kind of face the kid was making.

'Pat,' I shouted – yes, I guess I shouted. 'Do me a favour and take that boy away, take him away,' I shouted. 'I can't stand it, that face, those grateful eyes, all for two packs of cigarettes, I can't stand it – I tell you, it's as if I'd given him the whole world. Pat,' I shouted, 'take him away, and make him a parcel of everything we've got here, pack it all up and give it to him!'

Jesus, was I glad when Pat left with the kid. Pat'll make him a nice big parcel, I thought; and there you sat beside the dirty grey water, chatting a bit with the river all because of some skinny girl's face and thinking: throw yourself in, throw yourself in, let yourself be carried all the way to . . . ha, Holland, for Christ's sake! But that child threw himself in, splash! threw himself in because of a few scraps of paper that were worth maybe less than a dollar.

The Green Silk Shirt

I did exactly as I had been told: without knocking I pushed open the door and walked in. But then it was a shock suddenly to find myself confronting a tall, stout woman whose face had something strange about it, a fantastic complexion: it was healthy, it positively shone with health, calm and confident.

The expression in her eyes was cold; she was standing at the table cleaning vegetables. Beside her was a plate with the remains of a pancake which a big fat cat was sniffing at. The room was cramped and low-ceilinged, the air stale and greasy. A sharp, choking bitterness caught at my throat while my shy gaze roamed restlessly between pancake, cat and the woman's healthy face.

'What d'you want?' she asked without looking up.

With trembling hands I undid the clasp of my briefcase, hitting my head against the low doorframe; finally I brought the object to light: a shirt.

'A shirt,' I said huskily, 'I thought . . . perhaps . . . a shirt.'

'My husband has enough shirts for ten years!' But then she raised her eyes as if by chance, and her gaze fastened on the soft, rustling, green shirt. When I saw an ungovernable craving flare up in her eyes, I was sure the battle was won. Without wiping her fingers, she grabbed the shirt, holding it up by the shoulders; she turned it round, examined every seam, then muttered something indistinguishable. Impatient and anxious, I watched her go back to her cabbage, cross to the stove, and lift the lid of a sizzling saucepan. The aroma of hot, good-quality fat spread through the room.

145

Meanwhile the cat had been sniffing at the pancake, apparently not finding it good or fresh enough. With a lazy, graceful leap, the cat jumped onto the chair, from the chair onto the floor, and slipped past me through the door.

The fat bubbled, and I thought I could hear the crackling bits of bacon hopping about under the saucepan lid, for by this time some ancient memory had told me that it was bacon, bacon in that saucepan. The woman went on scrubbing her cabbage. Somewhere outside a cow was lowing softly, a cart creaked, and still I stood there at the door while my shirt dangled from a dirty chairback, my beloved, soft, green silk shirt, for whose softness I had been longing for seven years . . .

I felt as if I were standing on a red-hot grill while the silence oppressed me unutterably. By now the pancake was covered by a black cloud of sluggish flies: hunger and revulsion, a dreadful revulsion, combined in an acrid bitterness that closed my throat; I began to sweat.

At last I reached out hesitantly for the shirt. 'You,' I said, my voice even huskier than before, 'you . . . don't want it?'

'What d'you want for it?' she asked coldly, without looking up. Her quick, deft fingers had finished cleaning the cabbage; she placed the leaves in a colander, ran water over them, stirred them all under the water, then again lifted the lid of the saucepan where the bacon was sizzling. She slid the leaves into the saucepan, and the delicious hiss again revived old memories: memories of a time that might have lain a thousand years in the past, yet I am only twenty-eight . . .

'Well, what d'you want for it?' she asked somewhat impatiently.

But I'm no good at bargaining, no, although I have visited every black market between Cap Gris Nez and Krasnodar.

I stammered: 'Bacon . . . bread . . . maybe some flour, I thought . . .'

Now for the first time she raised her cold blue eyes and looked at me coolly, and at that moment I knew I was done for . . . never, never again in this life would I know the taste of bacon, bacon would forever remain no more than a wave of painful aromatic memory. Nothing mattered any more, her gaze had struck me, transfixed me, and now my whole self was draining out . . .

She laughed. 'Shirts!' she cried scornfully. 'I can have shirts for a few bread ration coupons.'

I snatched the shirt from the chair, knotted it round the neck of this virago and strung her up like a drowned cat on the nail beneath the big crucifix that hung black and threatening on the yellow wall above her face . . . but I did this only in my imagination. In reality I grabbed my shirt, bundled it up, and stuffed it back into the briefcase, then turned to the door.

The cat was crouching in the hallway over a saucer of milk, greedily lapping it up. As I passed, it lifted its head and nodded as if wanting to acknowledge and comfort me, and in its green, veiled eyes there was something human, something unutterably human . . .

But because I had been advised to be patient, too, I felt obliged to try again. If only to escape the oppressive brilliance of the sky, I made my way under crippled apple trees, among cowpats and busily pecking chickens, towards a somewhat larger farmhouse situated to one side under the solid shade of some ancient linden trees. The bitterness must have blurred my vision, for it was only at the last moment that I noticed a brawny young farm lad sitting on a bench in front of the house and calling out endearments to two grazing horses. When he saw me he laughed, and called through an open window into the house: 'Number eighteen's coming, Ma!' Then he slapped his thigh with glee and began to fill a pipe; his laughter was answered indoors by a throaty chuckle, and the shiny, crimson face of a woman appeared for a second in the window like a dripping pancake. I turned on my heel and ran like a madman, my briefcase tucked tightly under my arm. I didn't slow up until I reached the village street again and walked down the hill that I had climbed half an hour earlier.

I breathed a sigh of relief when I saw the friendly, grey snake of the highway below me, bordered with gentle trees. My pulse slowed down, the bitterness subsided, while I rested at the crossing where the cobbled, neglected, fetid village street emerged into the freedom of the highway.

I was dripping with sweat.

Suddenly I smiled, lit my pipe, pulled off my old, sticky, soiled shirt, and slipped into the cool, soft silk; it flowed gently down my body and right through me, and all my bitterness melted away, all of it, to a mere nothing; and as I walked back along the highway towards the railway station I felt welling up inside me a yearning for the poor, abject face of the city, behind whose contorted features I had so often seen the humanity bred by misery.

The Waiting-Room

At first when I woke up I couldn't believe it – no, it couldn't be true. Once more I stuck my hand out from under the blanket and took it back again. Was I still dreaming? It couldn't be true; could the cold really have broken over-night? It was warm . . . and mild; but oh, was I suspicious! I don't know whether you were also born in 1917 – we are a very suspicious lot, the survivors of that generation, as rare as cigarettes among so-called honest folk. Well, in the end I had to trust my senses: I got up. Yes, it really was mild, the sunshine was warm and gentle, the windows were entirely free of ice . . . they shimmered moistly, like the eyes of young girls who still believe in love.

My heart felt so light while I was dressing – what a relief that the cruel, murderous cold had broken. I looked out of the window: surely people were striding out more freely and happily, although the street was wet, but with a benign wetness, and from between grey clouds shone a moist sun . . . and yes, I could almost believe that the trees were turning green! What arrant nonsense, in the middle of January. But you see how little one can trust one's senses and how right I was to be suspicious; oh, careful, careful! You will find it ridiculous, but after walking only a few hundred yards I felt myself sweating . . . I really was. You will think: 1917, born during one war and cracked up during another . . . No, no, it's really true, I was sweating . . .

And I felt so light, the mild air and the sun and the dreamlike certainty that the cold seemed really to have broken made me reckless; at the corner I bought a good cigarette with almost the last of my money, pumped it

149

voluptuously through my lungs, and blew the thin, grey smoke into the springlike air. I responded with a regretful smile to a pretty, red-haired girl who offered me bread-ration coupons and the next moment I had jumped onto a tram passing at full speed. Wasn't there, in spite of all the misery, a gleam of relief in people's eyes that the cruel cold had been conquered by a 'warm air front'?

Didn't the sweet, tender air vibrate with sighs of relief? I even found a valid tram ticket in the depths of my coat lining, which meant that I could keep the fifty-pfennig piece intact in my pocket.

I smoked the entire cigarette without pinching it out. That hadn't happened for a long time – how reckless! I calculated in a kind of daze: since April 1945 . . . that meant for almost two years, since my first days as a prisoner of war, I hadn't smoked an entire cigarette without pinching it out. Was some fundamental change taking place in me? I spat the butt, which was almost burning my lips, out into the street. The conductress called out cheerfully: 'Main station!' I got off deep in thought . . .

What bliss, to submerge oneself in the bustle of the huge waiting-room! You will say, or at least think: how can a man who was a soldier for many years, who has had to wait to the point of stupefaction for so many trains in all the waiting-rooms of Europe – how can a man like that enjoy sitting in a waiting-room? Oh, you don't understand. In this swarm of harried, weighed-down fellow creatures who, in the aftermath of war, are travelling – must travel – to somewhere from somewhere – in the midst of this bustle I pursue the secrets of solitude, of that blissful solitude which I was never allowed to find . . . Here I can be truly alone, truly, truly alone and dream, dream to my heart's content. Silence is not for us . . . silence scares us; with cruel fingers silence rips off the frail blanket of stoicism that we have spread over our memories and thrusts straight into the teeming, bloodied darkness of our brief, pain-fraught life. Silence . . . silence is like a great snow-white screen onto which we project the joyless film of our lives. Silence can offer us no rest . . .

But here, in this impersonal hum, the ebb and flow of outlandish images, in the midst of sounds I do not hear, of apparitions I do not see . . . here there is a kind of peace, that's right, some kind of peace: here I can abandon myself to my dreams.

You will find this very foolish; but I have meanwhile discovered that there is nothing more pleasant than foolishness. Unfortunately we were never given enough time to be foolish . . . that was the trouble. We were too young when the horror broke over us, and now we are too old to 'learn'. Or would you care to tell me what I am supposed to learn? With that mild, warm air, hadn't hope reawakened in those grey, pathetic faces of the homeless?

I idly jingled my fifty-pfennig piece against a bunch of safety pins I carried in my pocket, a habit I had picked up in the army – I always have to carry some safety pins in case buttons are ripped off or fabric gets torn; a cheap little quirk, you must admit, not an expensive indulgence.

I drank my beer straight down; today the insipid stuff tasted marvellous – I was really thirsty; but what had happened to my appetite? I sat down on a chair that had just been vacated and wondered about my appetite, which seemed to have vanished with the cold . . . or had the cigarette absorbed it? I was profoundly shocked; where was my hunger, that faithful companion of so many years, that many-headed creature, often searing and vicious, sometimes just gently growling or amiably prompting: that mysterious monster that was second nature to me, fluctuating between wolfish greed and pitiful pleading?

One day, by the grace of God, I shall write a poem, a poem about my hunger. I became very uneasy.

Not only because of my hunger, not only because of this unexpected spring, not only because of my faraway, phantom beloved, perhaps unborn, or perished in the ghastly embrace of the war, for whom I sometimes waited here with a quaking heart . . . no, no, I was also here for a purely practical reason. I was waiting for Edi. Edi was to tell me whether the deal would come off; if so, I would be the richer by three hundred marks – if not, well, I wouldn't be. But if it did come off I could buy a violin, which I craved . . . it would make me happy, even happier, even freer . . . oh, a violin! I love music almost more than I do that faraway, phantom beloved, who, I often believe, will appear any moment in the door of the waiting-room, so that I look tensely and with a trembling heart in that direction . . . breathless and intoxicated by the thought that she has now become flesh and blood and will walk towards me with a smile.

So I was waiting for Edi. You may sometimes have wondered what people in waiting-rooms are waiting for! You probably believe that they are all waiting for arriving and departing trains. If you only knew the kind of things a person can wait for. One can wait for anything that exists between Nothing and God. Yes, there are even people waiting for Nothing.

My hair is now considerably thinner; illnesses, usually found only among the aged, plague me according to the season; and if I – please don't be alarmed! – take off my shirt, you can see some scars that might affect you like a painting by Goya; and the scars you could look at if I . . . but since you are a lady I will say no more. You won't believe that I finished school ten years ago, by the skin of my teeth incidentally, and that during those ten years I have never been out of uniform, except for the last five months, since my return from P.O.W. camp – and I have never hated anything in my life so totally and profoundly as that uniform! I didn't know what occupation to enter on my release papers. High-school student? High-school graduate? Oh, if only I could have said, with a clear conscience: labourer. But with thinning hair and at almost thirty . . . high-school graduate? It didn't seem funny to me – at that moment my eyes were opened . . .

It was the biggest mistake of my life to listen, against my better judgment, to the advice of so-called sensible older people who told me to 'volunteer': because it was inevitable, 'then you'll have it over with!' and so on. And the same people give me all kinds of advice today: learn a trade, go to university. Perhaps you will understand that today I am very suspicious of these so-called sensible older people who, after all – I should have thought of that! – are also the voters of those earlier days.

Waiting-room! By the grace of God I may one day write a wonderful poem about you. Not a sonnet. Some formless, ardent, passionate creation, as irrational as love . . . O waiting-room, thou art the wellspring of my wisdom, thou art my oasis . . . and I have found many a decent cigarette butt in thy depths when my heart was heavy.

I find the relative freedom of a civilian to be extremely pleasant and amusing; it is a glorious thing to be truly free, as free as a person can be without money. With money, of course, this freedom would have an even more golden face.

Don't talk to me about careers! I'll get by . . . tramp, you think, gypsy? So what? Do you find that very anti-social? So what? . . . I won't go under that easily.

Even in the waiting-room the air was – yes, lighter, I'd say. Hadn't the burden of those terrible hours of waiting been lightened for the travellers now that the icy cold had disappeared overnight as if by magic? And yet there was this waiting, waiting . . .

There are even some people who await something – note the difference between waiting and awaiting. Waiting is the condition of a certain impatient hopelessness; awaiting is an expectant certainty: slack sails are filled with the intoxicating breath of hope.

But Edi didn't turn up. I became impatient, restless. Oh, if only I hadn't involved myself in this deal! Time and again I regretted it, and time and again I fell for it; you sell all your freedom when you begin to make deals. Involuntarily, you think of some stupid 'compensation', as they call it . . . it bores its way, deeper and deeper, gnawing like a worm at the precious peace of dreams and freedom. Always that net you have to slip through. I made up my mind never to get involved in such things again. Why not simply take up begging? How wonderful to be able to rattle off some phrase or other that would yield a modicum of bread and cash.

Of course Edi didn't turn up. Not that he is unreliable: I know him well – we spent many a dark Russian night together in cold and heat, in the dark womb of the earth which is the infantry's element. Edi is quite a smart fellow, although he has been laughing at me for as long as we've known each other, and although he is just a shade too dressy for my taste. But he's loyal. He found me a place when I returned from P.O.W. camp, and he kept my head above water for those first few weeks. And he is reliable. If he doesn't turn up, there must be some good reason . . .

154

perhaps they had caught him – who knows? – he's probably involved in all sorts of murky deals I know nothing about; his hands often tremble so strangely, he seems so jittery. And how calm he always used to be! Nothing could faze him or frighten him. But this strange peace in which we children of the war find ourselves has utterly corrupted Edi; he is sinking, I can feel it; he's gradually going under . . . the temptation to become unscrupulous is so great that scarcely anyone can resist it. Oh, Edi . . . I shall tell him, in a calm and friendly manner, that I won't make any more deals with him, not even the so-called legitimate ones.

Ah, my beloved . . . my faraway, faraway darling dove . . . if only you were here! Once again I plunged into that beautiful daydream, I cast everything away and went towards her . . . that faraway, nameless one, the only one . . . towards her, my only true home about whom, by the grace of God, I will some day write one last poem.

Suddenly I felt a rough punch on my right arm and I turned round, startled and annoyed. I looked into the face of an elderly woman who had apparently prodded me on purpose: I awoke to so-called reality, and the 'true' face of the waiting-room loomed before me: grimy, musty . . . wretched, ugly . . . worn-down, worn-out figures, loitering, squatting on bundles that looked as if they couldn't possibly contain objects worth keeping. But the old woman plucked impatiently at my sleeve. 'Hey . . . young man!' she said. I looked at her squarely; she was sitting on a chair beside me. Grey hair, a coarse, plain face . . . a farmer's wife, I thought. A grey-blue kerchief, a wrinkled face, swollen, work-worn hands. I looked up at her expectantly. 'Yes?'

She seemed to hesitate a moment, then pointed to the brown hat lying on my right knee: 'Wouldn't you like to trade it? I could use it, for my son!'

I was not surprised. When you spend half a day sitting around in waiting-rooms, you get to know the secrets of our so-called modern economy, based on the secret cigarette currency and carried on in the form of barter. I laughed.

'No, I need it myself – it's about the only thing I possess, and after all it's still January.'

The old woman shook her head with an exasperating calm. 'January!' she said scornfully. 'Can't you see that spring has come?' She pointed to the ceiling of the waiting-room as if spring were to be seen there in the flesh.

I looked up involuntarily; the woman had turned away and was digging into some piece of luggage lying half under her chair; in doing so she bumped a youth who was sleeping with his elbows on the table; he opened his eyes in annoyance, swore under his breath, then laid his head down on the table. A young girl sitting opposite me and reading a book glanced up; with a frown she looked at the woman and me and went on reading. The old woman had finally dug out what she was looking for, and her coarse fists placed a big round loaf of bread, brown bread, between us on the table.

'I'd give you that for it,' she said stolidly. I have no doubt the look I gave the bread sealed the fate of my hat. I'm no good at bargaining. I know – I should have pretended to be stand-offish, should have ignored the bread, but I'm no good at bargaining, as I told you before. And besides – at the sight of the crusty brown bread my hunger was back again. In less than no time there it suddenly was beside me, this time wagging its tail and barking with pleasure, like a puppy whimpering expectantly as it sniffs at the house-wife's apron; with one astonishing bound it had come back from some distant place where it had gone off for a walk. All that was no doubt to be read in my eyes. The woman knew even before I did that she would get the hat . . . oh, that farmer's wife could write a psychology of hunger. How many hungry eyes have hung around her front door!

But I resisted. 'No, no . . .' I said fervently, and involuntarily grabbed my hat as if to protect it. 'No – for a loaf of bread?' My eyes flickered between the bread, my hat, and the woman's cold face. 'No,' I repeated, trying to give my voice firmness. 'Not for a loaf of bread!' The woman seemed somewhat surprised. 'Aren't you hungry, then?' What an infamous way to try and snatch my hat from me! For a split second I wondered whether I shouldn't grab the loaf, put on my hat, and make a run for it. But then I would never again be able to enter that waiting-room in a calm frame of mind.

I shook my head vehemently. The woman gave a little smile, a bit more lenient, it seemed to me; then without a word she leaned down and fished out a second loaf from the depths under her chair. 'Well?' she asked triumphantly. The light of victory was plain to see in her eyes. The thought that I had only to say the one little word 'yes' to gain possession of two fragrant loaves of bread intoxicated me. But had the Devil in the shape of a barterer's soul taken possession of me? 'You must . . . give me some . . . money, too,' I stammered, blushing. 'You . . . I'm unemployed . . .' The woman suddenly looked quite angry. 'Unemployed?' she repeated, dragging out the word incredulously.

I merely nodded, blushing ever more deeply, for the girl opposite me had once again looked up disapprovingly. 'Twenty marks,' I said bravely, staking everything on one card, and as if the Devil were really driving me I playfully spun my nice brown hat on one finger . . . for all the world like some careless youth. Oh, I knew it was a sort of farewell caress. The woman poked round in an old leather purse, grumpily picked out a few notes, and placed them beside the loaves. 'That's it!' she said sternly. Thus I was unwittingly thrust into the role of the person who is to blame for the deal, and the woman looked at me as if I were the most despicable swindler she had ever laid eyes on. Twelve marks I had counted with bated breath . . . two loaves and twelve marks, what riches! And how quickly I could calculate: four German or three Belgian cigarettes . . . two American ones! I stuffed the notes into my pocket, drew the loaves towards me, and quickly gave the woman my hat. She turned it round and examined it, her expression indicating that it was absolute rubbish, before it disappeared under the chair into that invisible container. I felt as if I were the lowest of criminals. Then my hunger took a wild leap over everything. I broke off a big chunk from one of the loaves and ordered another glass of beer from the waiter as he rushed past.

After my hunger had been fed its chunk, I was quickly alone again. In fact I even forgot that I had money for cigarettes in my pocket. The sweet grey veil of my dreams had been pulled across again. Ah, wasn't this a day when the beloved might arrive? Wasn't she on her way to me with her golden hair and black eyes, and with a smile that knew everything, everything . . . she was coming closer . . . closer and closer! Surely she was hungry! Oh, my beloved must be hungry, but I would not face her empty-handed; no doubt she was cold too, but oh, I would wrap her up in the warmth of this springlike day. If she was suffering fear and pain, my heart was open to her. I would give her my room, my bed, and I would sleep on the hard bare floor.

It was dusk outside and getting cold again; there was an icy draught round my feet and head. I looked desperately for my hat . . . oh, my hat! You won't believe it, but there was no regret in me, only distress . . . no, I did not regret having traded my hat, but it hurt me that it was gone. The cold was cruel, and it was a long way to my room with the bed where I could hide.

How infinitely rich I was in possessing a bed I could crawl into to escape the cruel cold. I would simply stay in bed; nothing and nobody could force me to get up. Mind you, there was silence there. But better to be exposed to silence than to the cold. Believe me, the worst thing is the cold. It crept towards me, across the stone floor and through the ceiling. What a nasty trick, to put on the mild, kindly garment of dusk just to pounce upon me again! I hurried . . . hurried out of the station, waited desperately for a few minutes for the tram, and finally walked home.

It was as if my head were gradually freezing solid, as if it were being showered with invisible ice. I had the horrible feeling that it was shrinking, leaving nothing but a tiny button in which a frantic pain was concentrating. What a fool I was to think that spring was here . . . it was January, bitter, stark January. All I could feel was that grinding pain in my head, but then it spread like some crazy turmoil throughout my skull . . . spreading, shrinking, taking possession of everything. In the end my whole head consisted only of pain and was growing tinier and tinier . . . a glowing, frightful needle-point drilling away at my consciousness, my reason, my whole being.

I believe I was feverish when (I don't know how) I reached home . . . I was feverish, haunted by dreams; my beloved was with me, but she was not smiling: instead tears were streaming from her black eyes.

And corpses were piled up round me like ramparts . . . ragged, mutilated corpses, some fat, some wizened.

159

When I woke again to so-called reality, I found myself lying in hospital . . .

Several times a day I would see round me those grave faces of the doctors who seemed to know all the secrets of life and death.

I had the dreadful notion that I might have woken up from my dreams wearing a uniform again. What was the difference between this hospital and a field hospital? No, there would be no more fever charts and grey-and-white-striped pyjamas for me. I am sure the urge for freedom made me recover so quickly that the doctors could congratulate themselves. I was well on my way back to health . . .

The day soon came when I could say goodbye to the nurse and shake her hand gratefully. I felt compelled to hurry, hurry, as if my beloved had now, at this very moment, arrived and was standing in the entrance to the big waiting-room. I had to hurry . . . but the nurse called me back. 'Good heavens,' she said, shaking her head, 'you can't go out in this cold without a hat!' And with a smile she handed me a hat, a blue one, nearly new, that fitted me perfectly . . . oh, I have quite a normal head.

Didn't it seem as if Someone were holding a protective hand over my head? Do you understand . . . ?

An Optimistic Story

Numerous requests to write a truly optimistic story gave me the idea of relating the fate of my friend Franz, a story that is true yet at the same time strange and almost too optimistic, with the result that one has a hard time believing it.

One day my friend Franz was fired from his job as a cub reporter on account of inordinate and insurmountable shyness, and he found himself out on the street almost penniless, hungry, and young enough to be desperate – all this on a sunny spring morning. I hope that the people wanting optimistic stories have no objection to a sunny spring morning, but for the time being, on account of his unemployed condition, I am forced to begin the story on a rather gloomy note. Franz was left with only fifty pfennigs. He gave much thought to what he should do with this. His most fundamental wish was for something to eat, for at all hours of the day and night he felt hungry, and his depression over being fired increased his appetite. Experience, however, had taught him that, to the very hungry, an incomplete meal was worse than no meal at all. Merely to stimulate the taste buds without satisfying them meant – as Franz well knew – worse torment than plain ordinary hunger. He toyed with the idea of appeasing his appetite by smoking, by inducing a kind of mild stupor, but then it occurred to him that smoking in his present condition would probably lead only to nausea.

Brooding over his dilemma, therefore, he walked past the displays in the shop windows. In a chemist's window he saw a display of indigestion pills, fifty pfennigs a package; Franz's digestion was in perfect order: he had none to speak of, in fact couldn't have, since these things do require some physical basis, and for many days Franz had been eating minimal quantities which had been totally consumed in his innards. Franz offered the chemist a mental apology, quickened his pace past a butcher's shop and a bakery, found himself, somewhat calmer, outside a greengrocer's, and wondered whether he shouldn't buy ten pounds of potatoes, boil them, and eat them with their skins. Ten pounds of potatoes in their jackets would certainly not give a mere illusion of satisfied hunger: they would actually satisfy it. But to boil potatoes he needed either wood or coal, as well as matches to light the stove; and since no one had yet thought of selling matches singly (here I permit myself to lay my finger on a sore point in the otherwise blessed and sophisticated state of our economy), the purchase of a box of matches would have meant sacrificing two pounds of potatoes, quite apart from the fact that he possessed neither wood nor coal.

There is really no need to list in detail the number of shops Franz walked past while a plan was taking shape in his head to buy a whole loaf of bread and eat it up on the spot; but a loaf costs fifty-eight pfennigs.

Franz remembered that he still had a tram ticket good for three more trips, with a face value of sixty pfennigs and a resale value of at least thirty. With eighty pfennigs he could easily eat his fill and buy two cigarettes. He therefore decided to make a clean break with his shyness and sell the tram ticket. Luckily he had just reached a tram stop. Studying the waiting passengers, he tried to read from their expressions how they would react to his unusual offer. Then he approached a man with a briefcase and a cigar, braced himself, and said: 'Excuse me . . .'

'I beg your pardon?' said the man.

'Here,' said Franz, presenting his tram ticket. 'Unusual circumstances, a temporary embarrassment, oblige me to dispose of this ticket. Could you perhaps . . . would you . . . ?'

'No,' said the man suspiciously, and with such finality that Franz immediately desisted. Blushing, he left the tram stop, crossed the street, and found himself in front of a newspaper kiosk. Here he stopped and started to read without taking anything in. He made vain efforts to tear himself away from the kiosk, and when the woman inside asked him: 'Yes, sir?' he knew he was done for, and with the last vestiges of good sense he named the fattest newspaper he knew, saying huskily and with an unhappy sigh: '*World Echo.*' He handed the fifty-pfennig note into the kiosk and received a forty-page packet of paper and printer's ink.

Aware of having committed one of the greatest follies of his life, he decided to go into the park in order at least to read the newspaper. The sun shone very mildly, and it was spring. He asked a passer-by the time and was told it was ten o'clock.

Seated in the park were pensioners, a few young mothers with children, and some unemployed. Noisy children were fighting over places in the sandbox; dogs were scuffling over bits of discarded greasy paper; the young mothers threatened and called out in the general hubbub. Franz sat down, opened his newspaper with a flourish, and read a bold headline: BRILLIANT POLICE!, followed by: 'Our police must recently have perfected some brilliant investigatory methods. They have succeeded in arresting a butcher for black-market activities. In view of the well-known rectitude of this trade . . .'

With an angry gesture Franz closed the newspaper and got up, and at that moment an idea came to him of such ingenuity that it may be regarded as the turning point towards the

163

optimistic part of our story. He neatly folded the news-paper, suddenly raised his hitherto shy voice, and called out quite loudly: '*World Echo!* World's Last Echo!'

He was surprised at his own courage and went on shouting, amazed that people took so little notice of him; even more amazed when someone asked him: 'How much for the paper?'

Franz replied: 'Fifty pfennigs,' looked into a disappointed face, and now had enough presence of mind to say: 'The latest edition – make it thirty, if you like. Forty pages, an excellent paper . . .'

He accepted the tiny ten-pfennig notes and, puffed up with pride, left the park convinced that everything would turn out all right. After briskly crossing a few streets he hopped onto a moving tram and remained surprisingly cool-headed when the conductor came round asking: 'Any more fares, please?'

After two stops he got out and walked to the station. Here he bought a cigarette for ten pfennigs, threw ten pfennigs into a beggar's hat, and with his last ten pfennigs bought a platform ticket. Smoking cheerfully, he passed through the barrier and fastened his attention on the Arrivals board. On discovering that a train from Frankfurt was due in one minute, he hurried to that platform. A voice over the loudspeaker said, 'Stand back!', and already the train was approaching. And when the train had come to a stop he suddenly had a new idea. Allowing his cigarette to dangle casually from one corner of his mouth, he ran alongside the train shouting: 'Hella! Hella dearest! Hella darling!' al-though he knew nobody of that name. He shouted implor-ingly, desperately, like a hopeless lover, and eventually, having run all the way from the engine to the tail end of the train, he abandoned his shouting and running with an air of deep resignation. He assured himself of a good exit by wending his way, heavy-hearted and defeated, among the parting couples and grumpy porters. He walked back down the stairs and finally spat out the cigarette butt that had been threatening his lower lip.

Like all shy people who suddenly discover their own courage, he had the feeling that the world was his oyster. From the Arrivals board he took in at a glance that the next train wasn't due for twenty minutes, coming from Dortmund. He decided to go into the station buffet.

Franz wrote me all this in great detail. These days he has plenty of leisure: somewhere in a foreign country he is living with an adorable wife in his own villa. But I must condense his story; I have been charged with writing a brief, optimistic story, for people no longer trust long-winded optimism, so I cannot describe the minutest nuances of every single emotional reaction, the way Franz did.

Let us hurry on, then. He entered the station buffet, buttonholed a waiter, and said hastily, like someone whose time is of inestimable value: 'I'm Dr Windheimer. Has Dr Hella Schneekluth been asking for me?' The waiter looked at him sceptically, shook his head, pushed up his glasses, and, disconcerted by the anything-but-shy eyes of my friend, said: 'No, sir, I'm sorry.'

'Terrible,' said Franz, and 'Thanks.' He sighed, groaned, sat down at a table, pulled out his notebook, which contained nothing, put it back in his pocket, pulled it out again and began to draw girls' profiles in it, until he was interrupted by the waiter saying: 'Can I get you anything, sir?'

'No, thanks,' Franz calmly replied, 'not today. I don't feel like anything today.'

The waiter looked at him again over the top of his spectacles and went off with his tray of empty beer glasses. At the next table Franz now spied a peasant woman with a little girl who, with admirable persistence, were eating their way through a basketful of thick sandwiches as if driven by a stubborn, proud, indescribably ennobling sense of duty to fulfil some loathsome task. They had not ordered anything to drink – thrifty folk.

At that moment Franz's hunger announced its presence with such vehemence that he couldn't help laughing, so loudly that everybody turned towards him – the woman, the child (both of them with a chunk of white bread in their half-open mouths), the waiter, and all the rest. Franz looked at a page in his notebook as if he had discovered something outlandishly amusing there. Then he got up, approached the waiter again, and said in a loud voice: 'If anyone should ask for me – Dr Windheimer – I'll be back in ten minutes,' and left.

Outside he studied the Arrivals board again and discovered to his horror that he had overlooked an arrival from Ostend printed in red. He raced over to the platform in question, saw the long, luxurious train standing there, was already opening his mouth, about to call out, when he remembered that he must use a foreign name, and he called out – no, he shouted: 'Mabel! Mabel dearest! Mabel darling,' and the result was what justifies me in describing this story as optimistic: in the very last carriage, in the very last compartment, at the last window before the pessimistically snorting engine, the head of a sweet-looking, fair-haired girl looked out, and she cried: 'Yes!' (in English, of course). Franz stopped in his tracks, looked her in the face, and said: 'Yes, you're the one,' and I must assume that she too, despite his empty pockets, found him to be the right one; for he ended his really disgustingly detailed letter with: 'We understand each other perfectly. Mabel is adorable. Do you need any money?'

I replied by telegram with the one word: 'Yes.'

I'm not a Communist

The bus always stops at the same spot. The driver has to be very careful, the street is narrow, and the bay where the bus has to stop is cramped. Each time there is a jolt that wakes me up. I look to my left out of the window and always see the same sign: LADDERS ANY SIZE – THREE MARKS TWENTY PER RUNG. There is no point in looking at my watch to see the time: it is exactly four minutes to six, and if my watch says six or even later, I know my watch is fast. The bus keeps better time than my watch! I look up and see the sign: LADDERS ANY SIZE – THREE MARKS TWENTY PER RUNG; the sign is above the window of a hardware shop, and in the window among the bottling jars, coffee mills, mangles and china a small, three-rung ladder is displayed. At the present time, there are mostly garden chairs in the window, and garden loungers. On one of these a woman reclines, a life-size woman made of papier mâché or wax – I don't know what kind of stuff they use to make mannequins. The mannequin is wearing sunglasses and reading a novel called *A Holiday from Myself*. I can't make out the name of the author, my eyes aren't good enough for that. I look at the mannequin, and the mannequin depresses me, makes me even more depressed than I already am – I ask myself whether such mannequins really have a right to exist. Mannequins made of wax or papier mâché and reading novels called *A Holiday from Myself*. It is all so depressing – to the left of this shop window is a pile of rubble on which mounds of garbage and ashes lie smouldering in the sun. It depresses me to see the mannequin right next to them.

168

But what interests me most is the ladders. We really should have a ladder. In the cellar we have shelves for our preserves, and the shelves are very high because the cellar is narrow and we have to make the best use of the space. The shelves are poorly made. I nailed them together out of some boards and fastened the whole thing with a piece of thick rope to the gas pipes that run through our cellar. If they were not firmly fastened, I am sure they would collapse under the weight of the jars.

My wife does a lot of bottling. In summer there is a constant smell of freshly boiled cucumbers, cherries, plums and rhubarb. For days on end the smell of hot vinegar permeates our home – it almost makes me ill, but I do see that we need the preserves. The shelves are very high, and on the top shelf are the cherries and peaches we eat on Sundays in winter. On Saturdays my wife always has to climb up there, and she usually stands on an old wooden crate. Last spring my wife fell through a crate like that and had a miscarriage. I wasn't there, of course, and she lay in the cellar bleeding and calling for help until someone found her and took her to hospital.

On Saturday afternoon I went to the hospital and took my wife some flowers: we just looked at each other, and my wife cried – she cried for a long time. It would have been our third, and we had always talked about how we would manage with three children in two rooms. It is bad enough having to live in two rooms with only two children. I know there are worse things – there are people living six or eight to a room. But it is also hard to manage with two children in two rooms on the same floor as three other parties who have no children. That's hard. I don't want to complain – I'm not a Communist, for heaven's sake, but it's really hard.

I'm tired when I come home and I'd like to have half an hour's peace and quiet, only half an hour to eat my supper, but just when I get there they're not quiet and then I smack them – and later, when they're in bed, I feel sorry. Then I sometimes stand beside their bed and look at them, and at such moments I am sometimes a Communist . . . Don't tell anyone – it's only for a few moments, you see.

Every evening, when the bus stops, I feel a jolt and look to my left: the suntanned face of the mannequin in the swimsuit is half hidden by the sunglasses, but the title of the book is clearly visible: *A Holiday from Myself*. Maybe one day I'll get off and look for the name of the author. And above the shop window hangs a sign: LADDERS ANY SIZE – THREE MARKS TWENTY PER RUNG. Our ladder would have to have three rungs, that would be nine marks sixty. No matter how much I juggle the figures I can't come up with nine marks sixty. Now it's summer anyway, and it'll be November before my wife begins climbing onto the crate again on Saturdays to bring down a jar of peaches or cherries for Sunday – not till November. So there's plenty of time.

But my wife is expecting again. Don't tell any of our relatives, and please don't tell the people on our floor. There'll be trouble, and I don't want any trouble. All I want is half an hour's peace and quiet a day. The relatives will be angry when they hear that my wife's expecting – and the people on our floor will be even angrier, and I'll start smacking the children again – and then I'll feel sorry again, and at night when they're asleep I'll stand beside their bed and for a few moments be a Communist. It's all so pointless – I'll try not to think about it again till November. I'll look at the mannequin reclining on the lounger

reading a novel called *A Holiday from Myself* – that mannequin right beside the pile of rubble and the mounds of ashes
from which a dirty yellow stream flows into the gutter
whenever it rains.

Contacts

Not long ago my wife met the mother of a young girl who cuts the nails of a cabinet minister's daughter. The toenails. There is now great excitement in our family. Formerly we had no contacts whatever, but now we have contacts, contacts that are not to be underestimated. My wife takes this girl's mother flowers and chocolates. The flowers and the chocolates are accepted with thanks although also with some reserve. Since knowing this woman we have been feverishly wondering what position we should propose for me when we reach the point of meeting the girl herself. So far we have never seen her; she is rarely at home, moves of course only in government circles, and has a charming flat in Bonn: two rooms, kitchen, bath, balcony. But nevertheless there is talk that she will soon be available. I am very curious about her and, needless to say, will behave with due humility, though also with determination. It is my belief that in government circles humble determination is appreciated, and it is said that the only people who stand a chance are those who are convinced of their own ability. I am trying to be convinced of my abilities, and I soon will be. Still, wait and see.

To begin with, our credit has improved since it has become known that we have contacts in government circles. The other day I heard a woman in the street say to another: 'Here comes Mr B, he has contacts with A.' She said it very quietly but so that I should and could hear it, and as I walked past the ladies they smiled sweetly. I nodded condescendingly. Our grocer, who until now had reluctantly allowed us very limited credit and, with a suspi-

cious expression, watched margarine, grey bread and cigarette tobacco disappear into my wife's shopping bag, now
smiles when we arrive and offers us delicacies the taste of
which we had forgotten: butter, cheese and real coffee. He
says: 'Now wouldn't you like some of this magnificent
Cheddar?' And when my wife hesitates, he says: 'Do take
some!', then lowers his eyes and grins discreetly. My wife
takes some. But yesterday my wife heard him whisper to
another woman: 'The Bs are related to A!' It's uncanny the
way rumours get round. In any event, we eat butter and
cheese on our bread – no longer grey bread – and drink real
coffee while waiting somewhat tensely for the appearance
of the girl who cuts the nails of the cabinet minister's
daughter. The toenails. The girl has not turned up yet,
and my wife is growing uneasy, although the girl's
mother, who meanwhile appears to have developed a
fondness for my wife, reassures her and says: 'Just be
patient.' But our patience is wearing thin since we have
been making ample use of that tacit credit which has
recently been granted us.

The daughter whose toenails our young lady cuts is the
minister's favourite daughter. She is studying history of art
and is said to be extremely talented. I can believe it. I can
believe anything, yet I tremble because the young pedicurist from Bonn still hasn't turned up. We look up ency-
clopedias and all available biological textbooks in order to
gather information on the natural growth rate of toenails,
and we discover that it is minimal. So this minister's
daughter cannot be the only one. Our young pedicurist
probably grasps one toe of Bonn society after another in
her adorable hands and removes the burden of dead cells
that can pose a threat to nylon stockings and ministerial
socks.

I hope her scissors don't slip. I tremble at the thought that she might hurt the minister's daughter. Female art historians have terribly sensitive toenails (I once was in love with an art historian and, on throwing myself at her feet, accidentally leaned my elbow on her toes, without dreaming they could be so sensitive; all was over, and since that day I have known how sensitive are the toes of female art historians). The young girl must be careful; the influence of the daughter on the minister and of the pedicurist on the daughter (who is suspected of social ambitions) is said to be extraordinarily great; and the pedicurist's mother had hinted (everything is hinted) that her daughter has already managed to secure a position for a young man of her acquaintance as clerk in the outer office of a departmental head. 'Departmental head' were the magic words for me. The very thing.

Meanwhile the mother of the young lady continues to accept flowers and chocolates with the same kindly smile: we are glad to make this sacrifice on the altar of high society, while we tremble: our credit keeps rising, and people are whispering that I am an illegitimate son of A's.

We have advanced from butter and cheese to pâté and goose-liver sausage; we no longer roll our own but smoke only the better brands. And we are informed: the young lady from Bonn is coming! She actually arrives! She arrives in the car of a secretary of state whose toes she is said to have rid of a whole colony of sinister corns. So be prepared: she is about to appear!

We spent three days in a state of extreme nervousness, and instead of ten-pfennig cigarettes we now smoke fifteen-pfennig cigarettes, since they do a better job of calming our nerves. I shave twice a day, whereas I used to shave twice a week as befits any normal unemployed person. But I have long ceased to be a normal unemployed person. We copy testimonials, over and over again, each one neater and more cogent than the last, type out *curricula vitae* (eighteen copies to be on the safe side), and rush off to have them notarized: a whole stack of paper will supply information on the tremendous capabilities that predestine me for the position of clerk in the outer office of a department head.

Friday and Saturday go by while we consume (on credit, of course) a quarter of a pound of coffee and a package of fifty fifteen-pfennig cigarettes a day. We try to converse in a jargon that might conceivably correspond to government circles. My wife says: 'I'm really so down, dahling,' and I reply: 'Sorry, dahling, must stick it out.' And we actually do stick it out until the following Sunday. Sunday afternoon we are invited for tea with the young lady (a reciprocal gesture for those twelve bouquets and five boxes of chocolates). Her mother has assured us that I would spend at least eight minutes alone with her. Eight minutes. I buy two dozen plump pink carnations – three for each minute: magnificent specimens of carnations, so plump and pink they seem about to burst. They look like the essence of rococo ladies. I also buy a delightful box of chocolates and ask my friend to drive us there in his car. We drive to the house, honk like mad, and my wife, who is pale with excitement, keeps whispering: 'I'm really so down, dahling, so down.'

The young lady looks delightful, slender and self-assured, quite the government pedicurist, yet she is gracious and charming, although a little reserved. She sits enthroned at the head of the table, fussed over by her mother, and I am dismayed to count seven persons at the table: three young scoundrels with their wives and an elderly gentleman who is kind enough audibly to admire my flowers – but our chocolate box is really delightful, it is made of smooth gold cardboard, has a lovely pink pompon on top, and altogether looks more like an exquisite powder box than a box of chocolates: this box, too, is audibly admired by the elderly gentleman (I am deeply grateful to him for this), and during the introductions I notice that the mother says to her daughter: 'Mr B and wife,' then after a pause, with more emphasis: 'Mr B.' The young lady throws me a meaningful glance, nods and smiles, and I can feel myself turning pale: I feel that I am the favourite and now accept the presence of those three young scoundrels and their wives with a smile.

The tea party progresses somewhat stiffly: first we discuss the enormous advances in the chocolate industry since the currency reform, a conversation prompted by a chocolate box that seems to have caught the fancy of the elderly gentleman. I have a dark suspicion that he has been invited to the tea party by the mother for tactical reasons. But for my taste the old fellow is too blatant about it, too undiplomatic, and the other three scoundrels, whose chocolate boxes remain ignored, give a bitter-sweet smile and the tea party progresses stiffly until the young lady takes out a cigarette: a ten-pfennig one, and embarks on some delicate government gossip. We spring to our feet, all five of us, to offer her a light, but she accepts only mine. I can feel my chest swelling and begin to have visions of my office in Bonn: red leather armchairs, cinnamon-coloured curtains, fabulous filing cabinets and, as my superior, a retired colonel who for sheer compassion can hardly see straight . . .

Suddenly the young lady has vanished, and for a while I fail to notice the signals of her mother who is trying to convey to me that I should leave the room, until my wife nudges me and whispers: 'Idiot – out!'

Breathing heavily, I go out of the room. My conversation with the young lady is carried on in a completely down-to-earth, businesslike manner. She receives me in the drawing-room, looks with a sigh at her watch, and I realize that some of the eight minutes have already passed – probably half of them. As a result, my speech, which I cautiously begin with 'Sorry,' turns out to be somewhat confused, but she smiles in spite of it all, accepts my gift of three English pound notes, and finally says: 'Please don't overestimate my influence – I'm willing to try simply because I'm convinced of your abilities. You will receive an answer in about three months.' A glance she casts at her watch tells me that it is time for me to leave. I toy briefly with the notion of kissing her hand, but refrain, whisper my most humble thanks, and stagger out. Three months. Incidentally, she was pretty.

I return to the tea party and on the faces of the three young scoundrels, whose chocolates were almost totally ignored, I discern poisonous envy. Soon there is an impatient honking outside, and the young lady's mother announces that her daughter has been summoned back to Bonn by telegraph in order to relieve the cabinet minister of his calluses; his golf game was to begin at nine tomorrow morning and it was already five o'clock, and with those calluses he would not be able to play. We look out into the street to see the minister's car; it is powerful but not particularly elegant. The young lady leaves the house with a charming little leather case and a briefcase. The tea party breaks up.

When we get home my wife, who has taken careful note of everything, tells me that I was the only one to be alone with 'her'. The question as to what 'she' is like, I answer with: 'Charming, my dear, quite charming.'

177

I do not tell my wife about the three-month waiting period. Instead I discuss with her what further courtesies we can show 'her'. My idea of offering 'her' three months' salary is rejected by my wife as an appalling lack of good taste. We finally agree on a motor scooter to be delivered to her anonymously but in such a way that she will know who sent it. Surely she would find it practical if she were motorized and would be able to ride from house to house with her charming little leather case. If she succeeds in treating the cabinet minister successfully (the fellow seems to have an advanced case of fallen arches), perhaps my intolerable waiting period of three months will be curtailed. Three months is more than I can manage, our credit is not all that great – I hope that the motor scooter, which I shall buy on instalments, will tip the balance, and that after only one month I will be sitting in those red leather armchairs. For the time being we both – my wife and I – feel completely down, and we sincerely regret that there is no such thing as an eighteen-pfennig cigarette – that would now be the very thing for our nerves . . .

At the Border

At the time, when I declared my desire to join the Customs service, the whole family was indignant. Only Uncle Jochen was sensible: 'Go ahead,' he said, 'go ahead and join it.'

One must make allowances for a certain degree of indignation: I had completed high school, taken a few terms of philosophy, was an ensign first-class in the Reserve – and now merely wished to become a Customs officer.

I have an excellent figure, am healthy and intelligent; moreover, I have always been obedient, so my career was off to a good start. A sense of duty was coupled in me with what I would almost like to call a calm broadmindedness.

By the time I had completed my training period and gone home for a few days' leave, with three shirts, three pairs of underpants, three pairs of socks, a nice uniform and the title 'Customs Probationer', the family's indignation had somewhat subsided. My father unbuttoned a bit and was to be heard saying publicly: 'My son, you know, the one who was an ensign first-class – my son is now with the Customs.'

My first day on duty I guarded the barrier at Bellkerke. It was hot and completely quiet – an afternoon; nothing was happening and, although I was tired and moody, numerous thoughts crossed my mind. After being relieved, I sat down, put those thoughts into some useful order and wrote a short treatise: 'Possible Border Incidents During Border Duty', a completely theoretical essay, I must admit, but one which as a modest tract aroused the attention of my superiors. In addition, the essay led to my promotion (out of turn) to Customs Assistant. This proves that my studies in philosophy had not been altogether in vain. I was transferred to the internal Customs service.

By the time I next went on leave, the family was already completely reconciled. In my free time I pondered on a short treatise for which I had as yet no title. In bold moments I almost considered 'The Frontier of Philosophy' but, while I was still uncertain as to the title, the work progressed well. I submitted it for publication in *The Customs Service News Letter*, where, under the title of 'The Philosophy of the Frontier', it reinforced my reputation as an analytical Customs officer and resulted in my appointment to full clerk.

Meanwhile I expanded my practical experience and planned to add to my essay an appendix entitled 'The Burdens of a Functionary'. I had high hopes of this work: it was to show the complexity of our existence at the border as well as in the internal service, and to demonstrate that a uniform does not impair the free flow of thought. I wear the smart green uniform with pride.

Needless to say there is no dearth of envious colleagues, most of whom come from the raw ranks of the mere practitioners, crude types to whom the beauty of the written word cannot be conveyed. There are actually those among them of whom I know for a fact that they have never yet read the literary supplement of a newspaper. Not without a strong inner hesitation I have meanwhile started on a third essay: 'Safety of the Frontier, or The Frontier of Safety?' Into this essay, in order to stop the mouths of the envious, I intend to weave much practical knowledge: above all, my experience that it is almost always the diplomats and the riffraff who get away with it, and I have found that the riffraff smuggle so diplomatically and the diplomats so riffraffishly that I will take the liberty of closing my essay with the words: Germans, stay at home and make an honest living! Actually I cannot see why – except in wartime! – one should bother to visit countries other than one's own. French morals and English perfidy infiltrate our country, nothing else.

Under the influence of certain intimate occurrences, my appendix, 'The Burdens of a Functionary', became so copious that it almost threatened to turn into a little book of its own. But I persisted and continued my polishing efforts.

My promotion to inspector was made conditional upon demonstration of my practical qualities, and I did not hesitate to report immediately to the front line: I posed as a coffee buyer at a large West German railway station, penetrated the very heart of a gang of which I became a member, and gradually let the current of this gang carry me onward and upward. I slept in extremely dubious dumps, was obliged to consort – in the service of the state – with women as seductive as they were dangerous, drank with thieves, ate with sinners, smoked with criminals and played cards with hardboiled villains. Stubbornly, patiently, I soldiered on, towards the top, and one day – oh bliss of mission accomplished! – I could give the agreed signal: seventeen men, eleven women, were arrested, and among those captured was the head of the gang.

Although the security of commerce was not completely restored, it was now raised to a higher level. I was given special leave; none of the envious now dared to accuse me of inadequate practical experience. When shortly afterwards I submitted my just completed essay, my triumph was complete: I was promoted to chief inspector and am presumably justified in regarding my career as secure. Moral: let no one be prevented from following the career of his choice!

The Surfer

After travelling thirty-six hours the young man arrived dead tired in Cologne; it was a hot Sunday afternoon in summer. The station square was crowded; large posters and decorative banners proclaimed a pharmacists' convention. The young man plodded from hotel to hotel, moving farther and farther away from the station, and finally found accommodation at the edge of the old part of the city. The hotel clerk told him he could share a room with another gentleman who had offered to give up the second bed in his room.

The young man climbed up the hot, narrow stairs carrying his only luggage: a briefcase and a bottle of lemonade he had asked for downstairs. On hearing a grumpy 'Come in,' he opened the door; the first thing he saw was a small white table on which lay many little pieces of paper and a pile of loose, dark-brown tobacco. The room faced the street. The windows were open, the shutters pushed out, and in the wan light the tobacco took on a purplish look. Opposite the door was a mirror; the washbasin had a long, black, yellow-edged crack in it, and in an open wardrobe he first saw only musty darkness but then distinguished a crumpled raincoat and a shabby briefcase from which a leg of some underpants protruded. To the left of the door was an iron bedstead with a white counterpane on which lay a black jacket. He finally made out his roommate lying on the second bed in the shadows of the farthest corner: a stout, unshaven fellow, his blue and white striped shirt arching tautly over his belly. The young man took him for one of the many pharmacists who were filling up all the hotels.

He approached the stout, motionless figure, who from time to time puffed out clouds of smoke, and quietly introduced himself: 'My name's Wenk.' Without looking up or stirring, the man on the bed mumbled something that sounded like 'Welter' and 'That's okay,' and continued to drowse.

Wenk turned on the tap, placed his briefcase on the bed, hung the man's jacket over a chair and his own over the brass knob of the bedpost, and took off his shirt. He washed slowly and thoroughly, cleaned his teeth and shaved. Welter neither moved nor spoke. His only movement consisted of occasionally opening his thick, swollen-looking lips and puffing out clouds of smoke. On either side of the projecting shutters, the smoke rose into the white triangles of sky.

Wenk felt much refreshed after his wash, lit a cigarette, then lay down on his bed and fell asleep. When he awoke, he found the other man had got up and was shaving. The air had cooled off, and a light breeze gently swayed the shutters. Outside the street was still quiet; somewhere in one of the neighbouring houses a girl was practising an étude, appropriately enough for a Sunday afternoon. She played badly, with many wrong notes, and at one place where the young man expected a cluster of semi-quavers she invariably stumbled or stopped.

Welter was standing in front of the mirror, vigorously swishing his foam-tipped shaving brush around on his face. He still had his pipe clenched between his teeth, but it seemed to have gone out. His shirt sleeves were rolled up, and the movements of his hairy, powerful arms were brisk. Wenk got up, relit his cigarette, and stood by the window. The street was empty, grey and quiet; in the house across the street, a slight, deeply tanned man in a singlet was leaning on the window-sill smoking a black cigar. Farther back in the room he saw a woman in a red petticoat powdering under her arms. The girl at the piano was now playing a folk tune, but that too she played badly, although softly and almost shyly.

'I envy you,' Welter said suddenly in a warm, attractive voice, 'being able to sleep in this heat.'

'When you've been travelling for thirty-six hours . . .' said Wenk, turning to Welter, who was just wiping the lather from his razor.

'Pharmacist?' asked Welter.

'No,' laughed the young man, 'I thought you . . .'

'For heaven's sake!' Now Welter was laughing. 'Although I've nothing against pharmacists, in fact I wish I were a pharmacist . . . By the way,' he continued, lighting his pipe, 'I've also been travelling thirty-six hours, yet I couldn't sleep – I wish to heaven I were a pharmacist!'

After so many hints Wenk felt obliged to ask, out of politeness: 'You mean your job's such a terrible one?'

But Welter was busy rinsing the lather from his face and cleaning his brush. Outside in the street it was growing noisier and, leaning out, Wenk saw what seemed to be a victorious football team in yellow jerseys, surrounded by a crowd of fans, pass by below. Across the street the woman was now leaning out beside the man. She was plump and young, and both she and the man looked bored. Welter had finished now; he was just putting on his tie and asked casually: 'Which route did you take?'

'Munich–Hamburg, Hamburg–Cologne.' Wenk had meanwhile removed his jacket from the bedpost.

'Good idea. Let's go for a bite to eat, shall we? I hope I'm not intruding . . .' Welter asked.

The two men spent the whole evening together; they

seemed to take to each other. They sat, drank some wine, strolled along the Rhine, and Wenk even persuaded Welter at one point to have an ice cream sundae. But he did not find out about Welter's occupation until later, after they had returned to the hotel. The wind had subsided, and beyond the shutters there was now a heavy, oppressive heat. They were both lying on their beds smoking. From the street came a mild jumble of voices and the sounds of turned-down radios. For a long time they were silent. Wenk smoked his cigarettes quickly one after another, hastily, greedily, until they almost stuck to his lips; then he would toss them across the room into the wash basin. The glow of Welter's pipe swelled from time to time in the dark, then contracted again, covered by ash.

'And why,' Welter finally said quietly, 'why have you been travelling such a long way?'

Wenk hesitated for a moment, then said: 'I've been following a woman . . .'

'Is she beautiful at least?'

'I think so, yes.'

They fell silent again and continued to smoke. From the hot streets and the scorching pavements, the heat rose in oppressive clouds.

'Ah yes,' Welter sighed. 'You see, I'd say you were twenty-eight years old, fair hair, about six feet tall. What would you do if you had five thousand marks?'

Wenk was silent, but the silence was suddenly different. 'Yes,' Welter sighed again. 'What would you do? The thing is, I'm looking for someone who's about six feet tall, twenty-eight years old, with fair hair. My boss relies on my intuition. "Welter," he said, "go and look for him. We must have him. Your intuition will help you." Oh,' he gave a scornful laugh, 'my own intuition makes me sick. In this heat everything makes me sick. But tell me, what would you do?'

Wenk remained silent for a while. When he began to speak, his voice was subdued, tired, slightly ironic. In the darkness he had flushed and was smiling. From outside still came that gentle, impersonal hum, and Wenk lit another cigarette. He said: 'I think I would do as they do in movies. Become a surfer or some such thing . . . Riviera . . . Florida . . . surfing. D'you know about surfing?' Welter didn't answer. Only the glow of his pipe swelled in the dark and subsided again.

'Just for once, to have no worries for three weeks or three hours,' Wenk continued, 'or three minutes, three seconds, like those rich whores with their johns who go surfing. Can you understand that?'

'Oh yes,' Welter said softly.

Again they were silent for a while as they smoked. Then Welter asked suddenly: 'You wouldn't take the girl along, the one you've been following?'

Wenk burst out laughing. In the dark he groped for his jacket, threw it across to Welter's bed, and said: 'You win, it's been in my breast pocket the whole time – it's all there . . .'

Welter did not stir or make any move to pick up or search the jacket. After a minute he merely asked: 'Do you think you'll be able to sleep?'

'No,' said Wenk.

'Then we might as well get started.'

In Friedenstadt

By the time I reached Friedenstadt, it was too late to phone Sperling. The station was surrounded by darkness, the little square filled with the kind of silence that even in small towns doesn't begin to descend until around eleven. Once again I had miscalculated, just as, while gambling that afternoon, I hadn't won, as I'd expected to, but had lost everything. To look up Sperling at eleven at night would have meant the permanent loss of his favour. That big hunk of a man, almost six foot six, slept at this hour as if pole-axed, while his brutish snoring filled the heavily curtained bedroom.

During the two minutes I stood hesitating on the topmost step outside the station, the few people who had got off the train with me had disappeared. I walked slowly back into the musty, semi-dark hall and looked round for somebody, but there was no one there except the man at the barrier, who seemed to be lost in thought as he stared out at the platform. His shiny cap gave him an air of solidity. I approached him; he raised a peevish face to me.

'Excuse me, sir,' I stammered, 'I find myself in a predicament. I wonder if you . . .'

He interrupted me, coolly waved his ticket punch past my nose, and said in a bored tone of voice: 'You're wasting your time – you can take my word for it. I haven't a penny in my pocket.' The expression in the fellow's eyes was icy.

'But . . .' I tried again.

'You're wasting your time, I tell you. I don't lend money to strangers – even if I had any. Besides . . .'

'The fact is . . .'

'Besides,' he went on imperturbably, pronouncing each syllable like a veritable lead weight, 'besides, even if – and you can take my word for it – even if I was a millionaire, I wouldn't give you anything, because . . .'

'Good heavens . . .'

'. . . because you've cheated me. No, don't go away!' I turned back and watched him take the used tickets out of his pocket and carefully search through them, as if counting the little bits of pasteboard like money.

'Here,' he said, holding up a pale blue object, 'a platform ticket, and it came from you.'

'Sir!'

'And it came from you! You should be grateful I'm not having you arrested, but instead . . . instead you're trying to cadge money from me. Don't go away!' he shouted at me, since I was trying again to sneak off in the dark. 'Do you deny it?' he asked in a cold, insistent voice.

'No,' I said . . .

He put his hand on my shoulder and took off his cap, and now I saw that his face, thank God, wasn't all that brand new.

'Young man,' he said, 'tell me frankly – what do you live on?'

'On life,' I answered.

He looked at me: 'Hm. Can one live on that?'

'Certainly,' I said, 'but it's difficult, there is so little life.'

The man put on his cap again, glanced round, then looked down into the black, empty tunnel leading to the platforms. The entire little station was dead. Then he looked at me again, pulled out his tin of tobacco, and asked: 'Roll or fill?'

'Roll,' I said.

He offered me the open tin and filled his pipe with his broad thumb, while I deftly rolled myself a cigarette.

188

I sat down at his feet on the floor of the little booth where he usually sits, and we smoked in silence while the clock hand over our heads moved quietly on. The soft sound came to me almost like the purring of a cat . . . 'Well,' he said suddenly, 'if you don't mind waiting for the eleven-thirty, you're welcome to sleep at my place. Where are you going anyway?'

'To Sperling.'

'Who's that?'

'A man who sometimes gives me money to buy life.'

'For nothing?'

'No,' I said, 'I sell him a piece of my life, and he prints it in his newspaper.'

'Oh,' he cried, 'he has a newspaper?'

'Yes,' I said.

'In that case,' he said, '. . . in that case,' and he pensively spat out the juice of his pipe, barely missing my head, '. . . in that case . . .'

We were silent again in that semi-dark, musty station hall where the only sound was the gentle, steady purring of the clock hand, until the eleven-thirty arrived. An old woman and a pair of lovers passed through the barrier, then the man closed the iron grille, plucked my sleeve, and helped me up.

By the time we reached his little house, Friedenstadt was enveloped in darkness, and I knew: Sperling's brutish snoring had now reached its climax: it would be roaring through the house, making the windowpanes and the house plants tremble, but I still had a whole night ahead of me . . .